RANGE OF LIGHT

RANGE
OF
LIGHT

A NOVEL

SCOTT NEUFFER

Livonia, Michigan

Edited by Jamie Rich
Proofread by Grace Nehls

RANGE OF LIGHT

Published by BHC Press

Library of Congress Control Number:
2019938913

ISBN: 978-1-948540-92-6 (Hardcover)
ISBN: 978-1-948540-93-3 (Softcover)
ISBN: 978-1-948540-94-0 (Ebook)

For information, write:
BHC Press
885 Penniman #5505
Plymouth, MI 48170

Visit the publisher:
www.bhcpress.com

Dedicated to Virginia Woolf, a true genius,
and to my daughters Emma Maria and Isabel Lynn.

"Less than All cannot satisfy Man."
~ William Blake ~

RANGE OF LIGHT

PART ONE

He wakes to the sound of the river running through the middle of the valley. A faint but persistent murmuring. The sound of eternity. Along with pines around his camp sighing, stiffening, in the first light, the wind. And birds starting in the thickets. Chirps piercing the air like glass tears.

He feels so spiritual in the mornings. Uninhibited. Free to roam the soft spaces before the chirps grow louder, heavier. But he wouldn't consider himself religious. His father was religious, but he never was. He left churches years ago. Whatever life offers him now—the rocks and trees, the light and wind, the sound of mountain water—he takes as enough. He wonders if a single flower is enough.

His campsite is close to the road. He's been rotating his tent between several sites to appease the rangers. Now, on the floor of his tent, he organizes his provisions for the day. He lays a pair of swimming trunks, a fleece sweater, and two apples onto a towel, folds the sides, and rolls it up as tightly as he can. He slips the bundle into his daypack. The supplies he originally brought into the park are running out. He hasn't fished as much as he thought he would, and he knows he needs more protein. Every other day he's been cutting open a can of tuna with the knife Red Cloud gave him. A bone-handled hunting knife with random nicks in the blade. It's become an unappetizing chore, eating tuna, and today he's heading up the mountain to see what he can find. Maybe a good fishing stream or somewhere off-trail where he can snare game in secret. He has no plans to leave the park.

He shoves a green plastic canteen and a water filter into the outer slots of his pack. Sunscreen and bug repellent round out the day's provisions. He zippers them all together. No camera, though. He doesn't have a camera and wouldn't want to take pictures anyway. He does have a journal, a leather-bound notebook and knife-sharpened pencil he takes everywhere. He keeps them together in the right pocket of his cargo shorts. Before leaving the tent, he finds the half-empty bottle of foot oil and begins rubbing some onto his bare heels, the arch of each foot, his toes blistered like tree bark. The oil smells of peppermint. As he slides dirty socks over his feet, thinking how he needs to do better with his laundry, too, he glances at the pair of briefcases wedged in the corner of the tent, covered by his flannel sleeping bag. Inside them, he knows, stacked like bricks, are two million dollars in cash.

Walking toward the road, he can see the cliffs of Yosemite Falls. The granite glows in the morning light like a painted backdrop. A cartoonish plaster of pink and gray. Black specks of birds twirl around the water's white threads. He breathes in the scene with a feeling of appreciation. The air fresh and cool and summer-scented. Then he stops beneath an apple tree. He grabs an apple and cleans it with the inside of his shirt. He bites into its pale, sour flesh. When he's finished, he tosses the core back into the forest.

In the parking lot along the road, he sees something strange: a woman approaching a deer with a paper cup. It's a young stag with fuzzy antlers, prodding in the fugitive grass between two cars. Though slim, the woman has the drooping look of someone in their late forties. She's wearing a short-brim cap of camouflage design, a blue tank top from which a white bra strap slouches, tight khaki capris, a tan fanny pack around her waist, and a pair of hiking boots he knows to be cheap. She's an attractive woman, and he feels a warm stir of desire. It's been months, maybe years, since he's had a woman, and he's forgotten the pleasant, head-emptying rush of arousal.

She's bending over in front of him with a paper cup from McDonald's in her right hand, which she offers to the deer.

"Come on," she says. "It's just water."

The deer stops nibbling on the grass and looks up at the woman. She steps closer, raises the paper cup, and shakes it in front of the deer's face as though tumbling dice.

"Go ahead, you precious creature. It's water. Just like you drink from the river."

The deer's eyes are round and bright like acorns. His hide and antlers are lighter variations of brown but just as bright. Used to the bizarre spectacle of human beings, the young buck suffers no fleeing instinct as the woman inches closer. His nostrils flare to smell the air. Her scent is strange. She smells like other humans, but also of something curious. Like something he once found swirling on the surface of the river, between the mossy stones.

She mistakes the deer's curiosity for fear.

"Come on, sweet thing, don't be scared."

She shakes the cup again.

"I wouldn't do that," the man says.

He steps to the side of her, realizing he's been staring at her ass.

"Excuse me?" she rebuffs, standing back up.

"I wouldn't try to feed the deer. It's not a good idea. That little guy doesn't look like much, but if you spook 'im, he could do some damage with that rack."

"I know what I'm doing. Deer aren't dangerous."

He laughs.

"Okay, but I don't think he's gonna drink from a McDonald's cup with all the streams and rivers around."

She looks indignant. He can see clotted redness in the corners of her light blue eyes, from allergies or sleeplessness or crying or some combination of all three. She has a plain face, with rags of ashy blonde hair hanging from the sides of her camo cap. Her mouth is petite and dainty like the corolla of a flesh-colored flower. It would be cute in a smile, he thinks, though her lips now bend in a frown.

"I'm sorry, I'm not trying to be a jerk, but you really shouldn't feed wild animals."

Seeing that the woman is ignoring him, the young buck nuzzles the paper cup with his nose. A plug of moist black velvet testing the glossy work of the logo.

Startled, the woman turns back to the deer, gasping in delight.

"See! You obviously don't know what you're talking about."

Disappointed with the texture of the cup, though, the deer turns from the two strangers and moves to another line of grass.

The man wants to laugh but restrains himself.

"I'm Stamer," he says. "Stamer Stone."

The woman feels the familiar burn of shame in her cheeks, her ears. She freezes with the cup in her hand as the deer moseys away. She wants to hit this man standing behind her, but she can't face him.

"You scared him," she says.

She throws the water onto the ground with the force of a shotgun blast. Then she turns to face him. She glares at him long enough to notice the wiry build of his body. He's wearing a floppy, sand-colored sun hat with a beaded chin strap that hangs unfastened against his chest. Brown cargo shorts and hiking boots make his finely haired, suntanned shins indistinguishable from the thousands of tourists in the valley, but the close fit of his gray T-shirt, the apparent firmness of his torso, and the veiny muscles of his arms suggest he's in better shape than most of them. She can see white whiskers in his beard, though he doesn't look older than fifty. His white face is not handsome by traditional standards, the nose a little too big, the grayish eyes a little too small, but it does exude a quizzical charm, a quiet confidence. She feels the first invisible tug of attraction. Like the buck, she has grown curious in a matter of seconds, but then remembers the empty cup in her hand.

"Whatever, just mind your own business," she tells him.

She heads off toward the restrooms at the edge of the parking lot.

"Wait!" Stamer calls after her. "Don't be mad!"

He follows her between the parked cars of the last row.

"Can you tell me your name?"

"Why do you want to know my name?" she yells back.

Stamer stops and watches her disappear around the corner of the building. With a random burst of energy, he sprints up the lane and cuts her off in the shade of the bathroom door.

"I have to tell the rangers who was feeding the animals."

She halts with spooked eyes.

"Hey, just teasing. I thought we had something going on back there, but maybe I was wrong."

"Are you stalking me? This isn't funny."

Stamer puts his hands up.

"Sorry, my mistake."

He backs away while facing her, hands still up. Then he turns and walks away, making sure she sees him shaking his head in disappointment.

She spreads toilet paper, as rough as sandpaper, on the toilet seat. No plumbing. A black hole stares up at her, exhaling a warm, noxious stench. She can make out lumpy deposits of black and brown eroding into pools of pulpy, murky green. The colors and textures and smells of a nightmare.

She pulls down her pants and sits on the crude ring of toilet paper, thinking she can prevent whatever's down there from coming up. But the thought of something biting her makes her cringe. She relaxes just enough to urinate.

"My name?" she whispers to herself. "Why would you want to know my name?"

Her name is Dorle Wasser. She is a forty-six-year-old waitress who recently lost her husband to divorce and her daughter to the courts. She presses her face into her palms, eyes closed. In the heated impressions, she sees grapevines, green stars cascading over each other. She sees the glistening floor of the courtroom. The polished wood of the desks and benches. The judge with his red face, his black-wire glasses, his stringy red hair combed over a shiny bald spot. *Chester Winfield is dead.*

"It wasn't my fault," she whispers.

• • •

THE CROWDS ARE GATHERING at the bus stop. Asians. Hispanics. Stinky Europeans with pink mohawks. Stamer has fallen in love with these visitors. He sees before him a great experiment of humanity. Every morning, the participants gather at the bus stop for the shuttle that will take them to the head of the valley. They come alone, or in pairs, or in groups, but each unit comes with its own aspirations for the day. He knows the relative strength of those aspirations will be tested against the constant variables of granite, trees, and waterfalls. The greater the aspiration, the greater the risk of failure.

"Good morning," he says to a group of Indian women.

There are three of them. A grandmotherly woman with a red bindi on her forehead and thick white braids that curl together like a cat's tail against the dark, withered skin of her neck. A motherly woman also with a red dot on her forehead and graying black hair in oval plaits that hang between the puffy shoulders of an apricot-colored blouse. And a daughterly woman with lighter skin and hair as black as coffee but no red dot on her forehead. They are dressed by degrees of generational decorum: the grandmother in a maroon sari that covers most of her body; the mother in jeans and the summer blouse that shows most of her arms; and the daughter in gray gym shorts that show her legs and a purple halter top that shows her shoulders and the naked round tops of her breasts.

"Where are you heading?" Stamer asks.

The grandmother bows her head, sternly, as if ashamed of the question. The mother looks annoyed but forces a smile.

"The Mist Trail," she says.

Stamer smiles back.

"I'm headed that way as well. Going to see the falls?"

"Yes. Vernal Falls."

"Well, be careful hiking up there. I heard it can be slippery."

"Thank you," the mother says.

She turns away from him, like she's shielding her family from further inquisition. Within seconds they're lost in the blooming crowd. Stamer imagines the grandmother's feet, the calluses on her heels and toes, a toothed, whitish crust over the dark skin. He thinks how she must have made similar pilgrimages in India, laboring up canyons of burnished stone, tracing sacred waters that run from the heart of the country.

He turns to face the oncoming bus. The crowds shift in an instant, just as the birds around the falls shift in the wind. He finds himself in the back of the line, falling back as more people surge forward.

"Excuse me," says a heavyset woman with a British accent.

She stretches out and waves both arms like a traffic director at an intersection. Her giant breasts, each the size of a tether ball, swing back and forth. Her head swivels left then right, left then right. Her right arm strikes the empty space in front of her, while her left arm drops behind and pulls forth a tubby man with cherry-red cheeks and a sky-blue visor.

"Excuse us for the commotion, my young man," he says.

He sounds like the cheerful keep of a backwater pub. His thick legs waddle without bending. His wife's enormous breasts swell against Stamer's chest.

"It's been a while since I've been called young," Stamer says.

The man grins, the crowd shuffles.

"Grab my arm," the man instructs. "Hold on for dear life. Mother will guide us."

As Stamer is dragged through the human menagerie he hears strange languages chiming in his ears. When the woman steps onto the bus, lifting the two men behind her, Stamer collides with a Chinese man. A camera falls and hits the road with a crack.

"Sorry," the man says, scrambling to retrieve the device.

"No, no, I'm sorry," Stamer apologizes.

He catches the heads of the British couple bobbing on the other side of the bus windows.

"Shit," he mumbles.

He moves himself and the man to the side of the door. The man is looking down at the camera in his hands the way a mother looks at a sick child. He blows on a fresh dent at the corner of the camera body. A quick interplay of his fingers produces a series of beeps and whirrs.

"I hope nothing broke," Stamer says.

When the man looks up, Stamer discovers a smooth and handsome face. Behind glasses shaped like inverted trapezoids are sharp, amber eyes conveying an unusual intelligence, a sensibility so refined and urbane that it seems out of place in the mountains. His thin lips look especially designed for a cigarette in a noir film. A wave of black hair sweeps across his eyes when his head moves.

"It's fine," he says. "It's a well-designed camera."

His voice is smart and effeminate. It sounds like the elegant smoke of that noir cigarette, if such a winding smoke could speak, or like rain falling on a dense city, hissing on a silk banner in a dark alleyway, or like a paintbrush swishing redly over a canvas.

Stamer remembers a business trip to China years ago. Rice wine and sweet dumplings. A restaurateur in a black suit and orange ascot, the latter like an exotic tuft of hair. There were dance girls and vague pleasures later in the darkness of the hotel, he remembers. The morning was a hot-orange cloud of smog. Then the runway, the metal jet a long glint against the plastic skyline.

"Digital?" he asks the man.

"Yes, a Canon."

"Here, let's get on the bus."

Their moment of intimacy collapses as hands and arms and elbows jam their space.

"That's all we can take, folks," the bus driver says after the two men have stepped onto the grooved metal platform.

The driver is a middle-aged woman with gray hair and glasses. She pulls the lever that closes the door with a hydraulic clunk. The two men move to the aisle, which is packed full of people both standing and sitting. With the same force she deployed in closing the doors, the driver now grabs the transceiver hung in a tangle of black cord beside the giant steering wheel.

"Keep moving to the back," her voice cranks over the intercom. "You in the cowboy hat, yeah, I can see you. Keep going, bronc buster!"

Stamer catches the driver's face in the oblong convex mirror above the windshield. Her face is a mean gray point in the shining bulge. He wants to pinch it like a zit.

The passengers plod toward the back, and Stamer and his new acquaintance grip the ceiling rail. The British couple waves from the rear seat. Stamer waves back half-heartedly, knowing he won't make it that far.

"You in the gray shirt, keep moving," the driver's voice cracks over the speakers. "Are you deaf or just ignorant?"

Stamer doesn't know she's talking to him until the Chinese man taps him on the shoulder and nods in her direction.

"It's okay, Jeremiah Johnson, I get paid by the hour, so I'll just wait."

Stamer's disoriented. His new friend has found a seat, but he's still reeling against the serried faces, the aisle, the gray point in the yellow mirror, more faces, then a man in a Smokey-the-Bear hat.

"You can sit next to me," the ranger says. "Don't mind Gina up there. She's just trying to make everyone's trip extra special."

Stamer laughs, uncertainly, and sits down.

"Randy," the ranger says, sticking out his hand.

"Stamer." He manages a quick handshake.

"Interesting name. Where you headed today, Stamer?"

"The Mist Trail."

"Oh, wonderful."

The ranger reaches down and tightens the laces of his hiking boots, twisting in a torsional manner as he works. Stamer notices the wool sock on the man's nearest ankle has slipped enough to show ghost-white flesh beneath the tan line, remarkably pale compared to the sun-darkened skin of the calf and the park uniform of khaki shorts and tan button-up shirt.

"Well now, ready for the trail—"

Stamer's not sure if the man is asking a question or making a statement. The bus lurches forward, and the ranger's head smacks the seat in front of him.

"Damn woman," he grunts. "I'll tell you something, I get real sick of her attitude."

Through the window Stamer can see Dorle standing at the back of the resurgent crowd. She rocks back and forth on her feet, smiles at random people—quick, fleeting smiles—and he thinks she's beautiful. Her image shrinks as the bus moves forward, then the ranger's hat blocks his view.

"Not going up to Half Dome, are you?" the ranger asks.

"No, not this time."

"Good to hear it. Had a nasty fatality up there a few nights ago."

Stamer heard about the death from other campers. Now he envisions the summit, the steel cables running up scoured stone like tracks of a defunct cable car, and finally that tilting head rush over the edge into some windy and godly view of the valley below—a perfect green gash where glaciers cut the mountain.

"Sometimes the summer storms come in quick," the ranger says. "The sky darkens. The darkness just falls on you. Well, the poor man was coming down. I was at the bottom of the cables, and I was yelling at him to hurry the hell up. Everyone else had made it down, and they were just hanging out. I guess they were waiting for me, even though I was telling them to go down the trail. Some were yelling at the guy. There were a couple college kids, too, gawking at me and gawking at the poor fool. They had the biggest, goofiest smiles. Their eyes were wild and giddy, like they were watching the damn circus. Then the lightning hit. It cracked and sounded like a million windows breaking. The currents chased him down the cables and caught him right in the middle. Everyone was shouting at him to let go, but he held on, even grabbed 'em tighter. He fell down on his knees, and you could see the electricity going through him. The currents were like snakes swarming him. He tried to stand back up, but they just kept pulling him down.

He started screaming, these horrible screams, and his head flung back to the sky, and you could see his teeth on fire. Well, I'll tell you something, that poor man lit up like a sparkler. Sparks were coming out of his eyes. You could smell him burning—"

Sparkler. That was the word Stamer was searching for earlier in the week.

He pulls out his journal as the ranger's still talking and finds the entry.

July? August? I know the year is 2011. I don't know the exact date. But I saw the light dancing on the water. It reminded me of—

"Can you stop now?" he asks the ranger, knowing the recent fatality was caused by falling, not lightning.

He's not sure why the ranger is lying.

The ranger's brow tightens, his eyes small and petulant. He has the same mean, pointed face of the bus driver, of authority petrified and unquestioned.

"Sorry, just too much for me," Stamer explains.

The ranger swallows a scowl.

"That's okay. Some people don't like a good story."

At the last stop at the head of the valley, Stamer exits the bus and finds a bench to sit on. He's about to start writing in his journal when he thinks of the blonde woman trying to nourish a deer with a paper cup. He chuckles with affection. He wants to wait for her but thinks how creepy it would look.

He slips his journal back into his shorts and walks toward the stone bridge over the Merced River. The bus-dropped tourists are creating a ruckus at a nearby concession stand, but the second Stamer steps onto the clear, uncluttered road he feels at peace. Morning light hangs from the boughs of dark conifers like lambent gauze. Streaks of light touch the forest floor. The trees themselves smell of Christmas, of summer, of Christmas and summer wrapped together. *Sparkler,* he remembers.

• • •

HE HAD ONE IN his hand and was running through the street. He was a
boy running through the street alone on the Fourth of July. The sparkler was running with him. It felt as thin as a pencil in his hand, but
powerful, like a wand, a fountain of fire, a waterfall of sparks. It was
hissing with life, the smoke thick and glorious, smelling like the barrel
of a cap gun or the tracks of an electric toy train. His wrist was loose
and rolling as he ran, writing his name with the smoke. S-T-A-M-E-R.
Stamer he was. Stamer he knew himself to be. A nickname? His real
name? Everyone called him Stamer. Because he stammered. He spoke
brokenly of the things he desired. Like the cap gun and the train he got
for Christmas. He couldn't understand why they broke. He couldn't
make them whole in his mind or in his speech. They were broken
things, broken nouns. Like the letters of smoke trailing behind him,
unraveling in the night air.

"Stamer, wait up!" a voice materialized out of the darkness. "I
won't tell your father, I promise."

The sparkler died with a whoosh. Stamer sprang around. There
was no one behind him. He'd left the yard without anyone seeing him.

"Who's there? K…Kristopher?"

The street was quiet. Cars on both sides like sleeping cats. And
the houses up and down the lane looked the same. They were the
square-and-triangle houses children drew in grade school. Each had
a chimney, a small stoop under the front door, a welcome mat, and a
narrow walkway leading to a narrow driveway. Each had a rudimen-
tary yard of grass and stick-figure elms. The older, lusher elms formed
a canopy over the feline automobiles.

"K…Kristopher, is that you?" Stamer repeated.

Looking back, at the end of the street, Stamer could perceive
flashes of light in his backyard, the hisses and pops of fireworks, all
revolving in the air like a noisy shadow lantern. Then the laughter of

children, schoolmates and church fellows. They'd been mean to him when his brother went missing.

"I'm not Kristopher, but I know Kristopher," the voice said.

"How ca...come I can't see you?"

"I'm invisible. You can't see me, but I can see you. I am your friend."

"My fa...friend?"

"If I weren't your friend, don't you think I would have scared you?"

"Wha...what's your name?"

"My name is Sparky."

"Spa...Spa...Sparky? Wha...what do you look like?"

The voice was close now.

"I look like Kristopher. We're the same age."

Stamer reached out and touched the air in front of him. He thought it felt like lukewarm water.

"Dad said K...Kristopher fell in the river, but I think he's in the fa...forest."

"I know where he is, but I can't tell you. It's a secret."

"Ca...cause he died?"

"I told you, it's a secret."

Stamer waved the dead sparkler in the air, slowly, wrist loose, swaying back and forth like a fish in the current of summer air.

"Okay, Sparky."

● ● ●

STAMER SEES THE CHINESE man on the bridge. He's leaning over the parapet, observing the clear, swift water of the Merced.

"I lost you," Stamer says. "I want to apologize again about the camera."

"Not a problem," the man says.

Stamer offers his hand, and the man shakes it delicately.

"Sorry, I didn't introduce myself. I'm Stamer."

"Li. Huo Li."

"That's a nice camera you got. A Canon, right?"

"Yes, a digital."

Stamer remembers the sound of the man's voice after their collision by the bus, soft and kind and intelligent, like the sound of the water.

Li raises the camera to his eye, rolls the focus back and forth between thumb and forefinger. He steadies his breath, and the camera snaps at the running water.

"It's beautiful," he says. "Impressive."

"How long have you been taking pictures?"

"Since I came here to America. I find everything here so impressive. Like this river. I'm not sure I could ever paint it. It's, how do you say, inimitable?"

"What brought you here?"

"School. A fellowship in Los Angeles."

"Engineering?"

"No," Li laughs. "Fine art."

"Oh, sorry, for some reason I—"

"It's okay. I'm from Beijing. Everyone assumes all we do is business and manufacturing."

"Beijing? I've been to Beijing. I worked for a firm in Vegas, and they sent me on a trip there. They wanted me to get a feel for the market."

Stamer suddenly recalls the downward pressure of the dancer riding him in his hotel room, how he gripped her gray, swany arms and came into the darkness.

"I'm not sure what you mean by the market, but it's very good our countries work together."

Stamer sits down on the parapet and pulls out his journal and pencil. Removing the ribbon bookmark, he stares at the off-white, faintly lined page. Then he scratches two words into the emptiness.

Sparkler. Sparky.

"I'm trying to write down some things about my childhood. I have this feeling I have to find something or understand something before it's too late."

Li sits down beside him. He reviews his photos on the small screen embedded in the back of the camera.

"I've heard this before, how Americans look back on their childhood for answers. In China, we don't do this. Maybe because we don't want to remember."

Li's softly ringing voice is a kind of anesthetic. Stamer closes his eyes and sees his hometown of Prideport, Pennsylvania—

How the town sits in a small valley between near identical ridges of thickly forested hills. How the valley is split by a large, rain-fed river, in some places the water as wide as a lake. How a bulky drawbridge connects the two sides of town, cranking, lifting for the slow barges heaped with iron ore, heading downriver to the steel mills. On the east side of the river are the neighborhoods, rows of small, single-peaked houses so similar that if not for the street signs at each corner, one street could be confused with any other. On the west side of the river stand the sharp steeples of the churches, the clustered stadium lights of the high school, the varied brick layers of the old-town storefronts. He's on the playground of Bredworth Elementary School. It's winter, and he and his brother are wearing hats and mittens as they slap around a tetherball. The cold air stings their faces, makes vapors of their breathing, and the ball chain creaks in its concentric revolutions—

"My brother disappeared when I was eight years old," he tells Li. "The whole town was looking for him. They had these long poles, and they were poking the bushes along the river. They were calling out his name, and I remember thinking they weren't calling loud enough. I told my dad Kristopher wouldn't be able to hear. He got mad and sent me back to the house."

"What happened?"

Stamer doesn't answer. He's a child running into the hills behind his neighborhood—

Maple leaves crackle under his feet, yellow and gold and scarlet, bright and crisp like construction paper, lying in tattered heaps at the base of each bare tree. Then a stream of clear water slicing open the hillside. It cuts through the collage of leaves with an icy precision that terrifies him. Up higher he finds a small cataract, a white flash in the fold of the hill, and below it a gurgling pool, swirling between the banks of leaves. When he puts his fingers in the creek, he can't understand the sharp, thrilling pain of the cold.

Then the sun is setting, and a gelatinous golden light begins receding from the stark, whitened bodies of the trees. It leaves an inky residue of shadow on everything, and he's running against it, scrambling up the crest of the hill, chasing the light as it shrinks between the skeletal branches, as it reddens and fades—

"It's funny. The summer my brother disappeared I had an imaginary friend. I could never see him, he didn't really have a body or anything, but he would talk to me. He would tell me that Kristopher was okay. He would tell me Kristopher was happy and having fun, but he'd never tell me where Kristopher was. Kind of screwed up, right? Even a made-up character in my head couldn't make up an answer."

Li rocks the camera against his stomach with one hand, tugging at the suede strap around his neck with the other.

"It's strange," he says, "about your friend."

"My dad was a pastor," Stamer redirects the conversation, as if memory were a river to be diverted. "He ran a small church in town. Fellowship of the Christ. Everyone thought Kristopher drowned, but we never found his body. That fall, we had a funeral for him at the church. My dad gave this speech that was just—unbelievable—now that I think about it. He was so mad, but he couldn't blame God. He wouldn't blame God."

Li makes a curt, dismissive hum in his throat.

"I grew up with gods in art and literature, but no *God*. The Chinese government discourages religious belief. We were taught to blame each other for our problems, not any god."

"Huh," Stamer ponders, picturing his father's church on the sparkling edge of the Merced, the arched doorway beneath the obelisk steeple, the shadowy aisle between rows of wooden pews—

The pastor stands at the altar behind a display of forty candles, one for each night Christ suffered in the desert. The candles blaze like a holocaust in the man's watery eyes, his hair suddenly gray, like wires of steel wool, and his face as wizened as a mandrake. Stamer hardly recognizes the face.

"The Lord," the pastor says to the tearful pews. "The Lord is good, but his children are not. The Lord is just, but the world is not. It all began with Satan's temptation in the Garden of Eden. Satan knew to prey on the weakness of a woman. In Eve, he saw the fall of mankind."

Stamer remembers that his mother squeezed his hand as the pastor said this. She was a quiet woman, soft-spoken, pretty, always pleasant in the background of his memories, except this one moment during the fake funeral of her first son. She squeezes Stamer's hand, and he looks up and sees her eyes are hostile. She's wearing lipstick, bright, searing scarlet, and the paste has slipped askew from the outline of her lips. The lips themselves are trembling, defiant. The image disturbs him. Both parents seem like strangers, transformed in their grief and guilt, locked like prisoners in a new dimension. She squeezes his hand but can't speak to him, as though the power of her new knowledge would destroy him.

"Man fell by the carelessness of a woman, but he was redeemed by the blood of Christ," the pastor proclaims. "It was a woman who introduced death into this world. Through her sin, she put man in an impossible position between his creator and his lover. She invited the Lord's wrath when she ate the forbidden fruit as Satan had tempted her to do. And through this act of weakness, she ensured death would have its day.

"Cast from Eden, man toiled in the earth all day and all night with the horrid knowledge that his life would come to an end. Even more than that, he knew all those he loved would die the same. And this death, this filthy, foul corruption of the flesh, gnawed on his mind all those terrible centuries. This putrid, sordid fact—it stank in the nostrils of the living, from Abraham to Isaac to Jacob. It befouled and belied all the laws and rituals of cleanliness. For death, my brethren, is a plague on the human heart. It infects the organ, taints the blood, makes men do things they would not otherwise do. Death is Satan's greatest weapon. It is death, and not Satan, that makes men evil. Satan only gives man glimpses, and these are enough to destroy him. Death is enough to make man steal for want, enough to make him kill for fear of being killed, enough to make him betray those he loves for fear he will not have lived his life to the fullest. It is death that wreaks evil upon the world, this germ born in the weakness of a woman. Death, you see, spins a shadow that ties all men together. They partake of the poison. They drink deep of life only to find ruin at the bottom of the cup. They suffer fever-dreams and convulsions. They spit up blood and clutch their sides in agony. For the lance has pierced their abdomens. There are nails in their hands, and foaming corruption at the mouth of every wound. Their bodies reel in pain and reject their own mortality."

The pastor hunches over the altar, his head crumpling on his arm, and the other arm clinging to the side of the altar like a serpent, the hand the snake's head, fingers biting the air. Then he lifts himself back up, tears cascading down his face.

"If only woman had considered man's faulty nerves, his fickle heart."

Stamer remembers the faces in the pews as quiet and blank as falling snow.

"But know this, my brethren, that man was redeemed by the blood of Christ. His blood was spilled so that man might atone for his sins. Through Christ's death alone, we may drink of the Lord's everlasting life—"

"Fear," Stamer tells his new friend on the bridge above the river called mercy. "My father was scared to die. For all his preaching, he couldn't handle the thought of death. My brother's disappearance just made it worse. He felt like it was an attack on his own existence."

Li removes the strap from his neck and sets the camera on the parapet over the water. He strips off a black daypack and then his stone-gray fleece jacket, tucking the latter into the former. A semitransparent, sapphire-blue water tube protrudes from the pack's shoulder strap, like an IV inserted into the hollow padding. Stamer notices how the pack conforms to the spine, slightly concave in the middle, matching Li's overall aerodynamism. It might look silly on someone else, he thinks, but Li slips the pack on with the ease and fitness of a fashion model. He's wearing a forest-green T-shirt, athletic shorts with a silvery veneer, and sneakers shaped like teardrops, as sleek and metallic as the shorts save their intricate network of neon-green eyelets and laces. In a nimble flourish he kicks one leg onto the ledge beside the camera and lowers himself on the other, stretching his hamstring.

"Death," Li says, "is hard to think about. My father never talked about it. But death was all around us. I grew up believing an individual life was worth little."

Stamer sees the streets of Beijing in his mind, cars and trucks and bicycles, more bicycles than anything, packed in rivers of metal flowing through the old-brick and new-steel canyons of the city, the air choked with fumes, thousands of people crowding the sidewalks, men in suits, women in heels, teenage boys with moussed hair and dressy shirts, cell phones sharp as rapiers, and shorter people, coarser, rheumatic, starved, millions of them in the interstices of the urban structures, in the corners and alleyways and basements. The harder he looks, the more he sees them, these steady, tired faces between the slick shows of modernity, not happy, not sad, but shut off from the rest, walking beneath the rest without question, working quietly in some invisible channel of time and space. They're like the steelworkers he knew growing up in Pennsylvania. He knows better than to underestimate them. Then there's a boy in a blue baseball cap. He speaks some English and asks Stamer if he'd like to see a secret door in the city. Stamer declines, but the boy grabs his hand and pulls him into the alleyways, clotheslines cutting the air diagonally, manholes clinking, geysers of steam, curs picking at scraps where corners turn on more corners, a turning maze of grayish brick, thick with the smell of smoldering particulates, until, breaking free from the boy's hand, he sees a red door—suspended like a pure hallucination in the drab walls of the inner city. It's beautiful, like something from a dream.

"In China, they trap you," Li says, watching sunlight dance on the river. "They take your life from you. It never belongs to you. Here, I think it's different. You can be what you want."

A red door. Something from a dream. Stamer can't remember how he got back to the thoroughfare. He's standing in a stream of people, dazed by the neon signage around him, the high, spotlighted platforms, the vertical, blinking banners of calligraphy. He pats himself down and realizes his wallet is gone.

"I'll have to tell you about getting robbed in Beijing," he says. "Maybe later. You definitely came to the right place to escape all that. This place is much better for thinking. Clean air. Wind and water. I've been thinking for a while now."

• • •

DORLE WASSER'S EARLIEST MEMORY is of a dark closet in her bedroom. Her mother had left the closet door open, and the rectangular black cavity in the wall became the image against which her brain performed its first act of retention. She still doesn't know what age she was when this memory formed, whether she was in a cradle or in a bed, but the image nonetheless haunted her youngest dreams. The gap in the wall engendered her first tangible sense of deficit. There was a wall, there was a door, and then there was this dark space between where neither existed. There was fullness to the door and the wall, hard and definite, and then emptiness. The emptiness seemed so big and deep. She remembers shadows stirring within it, so black they were almost purple, and the faintest tracings of some structural face, shelves perhaps, dimly edged like teeth.

She's sitting on a toilet in Yosemite Valley suddenly thinking of that closet.

"It wasn't my fault," she whispers again.

She stands, wipes, slams the toilet lid. She washes her hands in the cold, tank-fed water of the faucet. What's left of the soap is smeared on the narrow mirror, her face distorted by ribbons of oil. She sees her own blue eyes eaten by redness, veins knotted and inflamed against each crystal iris. She closes her eyes while spinning around to the exit. They water when she opens them outside. Sunlight flames through the trees. Her old bedroom flashes through her mind, jagged and purple like a broken window in the dark.

She walks through the forest toward the bus stop. She tries her best to inhale and hold the smell of the conifers. They make a clean smell, sere and sharp. She wants the smell and the sights of the park, the cliffs and cascades, to fortify her. Or annihilate her. She doesn't know which.

The man in the parking lot didn't understand about the deer. He didn't know she grew up in a white stone house on a vineyard, that a similar buck lived in a ravine behind the house, where a creek ran through glossy and tangled vegetation. Her father had seen it, the buck, the stag. Its hide was dark-red like cinnamon, its antlers fuzzy like crushed velvet. There were does lying in the smoothed and shadowed grass along the creek, under the trees. And a dark fawn, almost black, hidden between the does. She has a memory of feeding the fawn with a bottle of milk. But the memory is vague, a two-dimensional picture, a fading image. There's no texture to it. No associations with touch or smell. She wonders if her father invented the whole thing. The thought scares her: that a beautiful memory could be baseless. Walking through the forest, toward the bus, she then wonders if other people go around the same way, trying to fill holes in their being with memories and stories.

● ● ●

HER FATHER HAD OPENED the closet to show her the bookshelf behind the door. The faded editions, both hard and softcover, were like rows of brittle teeth in the square mouth.

"I don't read much anymore," he said. "We'll move these when you get a little older and want your own things. You might even want to read some of 'em."

Her father had a way of making his voice quaver when he spoke. And a way of underscoring his words with downtrodden gestures. A shrug of the shoulders. A fall of the hand.

"Your mother always gives me heck for reading. Says I'm filling up my head with nonsense. She told me I couldn't keep my books in the living room anymore. Of course she reads whatever she wants, fashion magazines and whatnot. I think that's the real nonsense."

He chuckled.

"Don't tell 'er I said so, okay, honey?"

Her father had a hard, pointed face. The tuft of graying blond hair on the bald summit of his head was a flag of his German ancestry. His brow peaked sharply, lifting his nose and mouth into a sort of snout, and his small colorless eyes blinked on and off behind an old pair of reading glasses. When standing, his body looked attenuated and bony, arms hanging at the sides, hands curved like pruning loppers.

"Daddy," Dorle said. "Mom said the house is old and full of holes. She doesn't like it here. She wants to move to the city."

The pointed face tightened until she thought it would burst. The entire head began to wobble.

"Sometimes your mother doesn't appreciate the life we have," he said in a cool tone, as though knowing she wouldn't understand. "It's not anyone's fault, honey."

"What's *fault*, daddy?"

"It's when you do something wrong. You say something's your fault when you do something wrong."

"What did you do wrong?"

Herr Wasser raked his forehead with his fingertips.

"I love you," he said. "That's all you need to know."

• • •

THE BUS STOP IS bustling with life—rude, incessant, squawking life. Seeing only dark, foreign faces, dapper and rakish with the day's ambition, Dorle feels herself as a frumpy anachronism in a racing modern world.

She's drawing her finger up the flesh of her right arm, catching the errant bra strap, when a bullish woman of middling age knocks into her.

"So sorry!" the woman cries.

"It's okay," Dorle says, lifting the strap again with the hook of her bare ring finger.

"I just can't help running into people. They're everywhere. Way too many!"

Dorle realizes they're near the back of the crowd, where there's still plenty of room for the woman to have walked around her. She wonders if the woman ran into her on purpose. She examines her with a quick rove of the eyes. The woman is stocky, sweaty, in her sixties, Dorle guesses, and she's sporting a bright-red T-shirt with an American flag printed in the center. The graphic is stretched ridiculously over the woman's large and sagging bosom. On her head, over dye-fried hair, is a denim-blue baseball cap, its bill folded into a triangle. Dorle thinks the woman sticks out more than she does; she rejoices in the thought.

"I guess it's all part of the experience," Dorle says in a dismissive tone.

She doesn't know why she's so quick to dismiss—what underlies this instant assumption of the other's inferiority—except that it provides the thinnest, fleeting sense of superiority.

"It feels like I lost the world a long time ago," the woman says. "This used to be a family place. Our entire family in Modesto used to come up here and enjoy these mountains. Now look at it. The place is overrun with foreigners."

Dorle reels back.

"Who are these people?" the woman shouts. "Where do they come from?"

Though she met the woman only a minute ago, Dorle flushes with shame and the guilt of association. She begins walking into the crowd, hoping to lose her, but the woman grabs her arm.

"Trust me," she says. "You'll want to wait for the next bus."

The woman nods in the direction of three Indian women, one dressed in traditional attire, all slowly being assimilated into the multitude of tourists.

"Look at 'em. They got the nerve to come here. Their husbands blow up our buildings, murder our children, and they got the nerve to come here like it's nothing."

Dorle is about to correct the woman's mistake, a blunder of racial profiling, but she stops herself. She realizes she's scared of the woman in the red shirt. Having led to condescension before, her instincts now urge her toward friendliness.

"I'm going to wait for the next bus," she says in belated agreement.

The bus before them gives off a hydraulic hiss. Two doors swish open like automated doors in a grocery store. In a matter of seconds the throng rushes forward, and the bus stop sheds half its population.

"I don't know why the libs go out of their way to coddle these people," the woman says.

"Everyone wants to come see the park," Dorle replies. "They believe there's something here for 'em. I guess we all believe that."

"It's revolting. They have no right to this park. It was built by Americans—for Americans!"

Dorle can't resist what she says next because it solidifies in her like a commandment:

"No, this park was built by God, by something bigger than us."

The pronouncement empowers her. She looks beyond the woman's perturbed face to the windows of the bus shimmering in the sun. The machine rumbles into motion. The sunlight becomes an inflamed line against which the windows flow like water. The light grows with intensity until it blots her mind with white heat. For a second, behind the burning veil, a man's face appears. A faint outline floating down the river of windows. There, then gone. The same man who'd approached her in the parking lot. She's already forgotten his name.

● ● ●

IT WASN'T JUST THE hole in the wall that scared Dorle as a child. She became obsessed with all spatial deficits in the house. Drains. Cupboards. Cellar. The latter was the worst. Her grandfather had been one of the first immigrants to bring vine cuttings from the old country, the Rhineland. He'd built the white stone house around a deep cellar gouged into the hillside. He needed the cellar not only to store future vintages—in catacombs he carved in the volcanic bedrock—but also to store root crops from the garden, carrots and beets and radishes. Everything, food and drink, would be kept in the cool, dark, porous spaces between planks of redwood.

To Dorle, the cellar was a crypt. The wood shelves smelled like what she thought coffins would smell like. The wine niches exhaled sour moisture. They dripped stains. Spiderwebs filled the empty holes, like woven nests. Where the vast shelving stopped, blackened timbers of the original foundation lay splintered against the dark cleavage of the earth and the crumbling stone footings of the house. She always sensed the world ended there, in the splintering textures of the foundation. She imagined being trapped, pinned in the earthwork, spiders crawling on her skin, dirt trickling through her hair. She imagined every hole in the house leading to this interment. Gravity would pull her down through the secret passages and slowly, atomically, entomb her. The cellar was the terminus of all deficits.

"Sometimes I think we should lock your father in the cellar," Dorle's mother said the day after she returned from the city.

She flashed a twisted smile.

"Then we could do whatever we want. I could take you to the city with me. You wouldn't have to be here all alone."

Frau Wasser had hair that was long and blonde and dryly luxuriant like the hillside summer grasses. She had skin white and smooth like the inner curve of a seashell. She wore storefront dresses to show off her figure, dainty arms and stem-thin waist. She wore pearl earrings everywhere, at all times. Dorle remembers asking if she could wear them, too.

"No, you can't. These are mommy's earrings."

Frau Wasser fingered the lobe of her right ear, delicately, warmly, as if remembering something.

"You'll get earrings when you find a man who loves you."

Dorle had seen the earrings the night before. Dorle and her father were at the table eating dinner when her mother walked in. She left the front door open, shed her coat on the floor, a woolen royal-blue long coat ribboning over the oak, and demanded her husband speak to her in private.

Dorle lowered herself from the table and ran toward her mother's legs. But Frau Wasser pivoted; in one fluid motion, she lifted her daughter in the air and set her down on the large square tiles of the foyer.

"You need to hold your horses, darling. I need to speak with your father."

Both parents disappeared into the bedroom. Soon their voices exploded against the closed door. Dorle remembers standing alone in the hollowness of the house, the walls on both sides of her amplifying the shouts coming from the bedroom. But she'd seen something in that moment her mother had shirked her—in the woman's ear a pearl as round as a marble, a drop of white fire, incandescent and shimmering. And as she stood there listening to her parents screaming, the image percolated inside her, tingling, filling cavities and crevices and corners with its fiery radiance. Its beauty burned in her mind.

"How will I know when a man loves me?" she asked her mother the next day, when both parents were calmer.

Frau Wasser smiled, not unlike the twisted smile she made about the cellar. "You'll know," she answered. "You'll just know."

She touched her throat in a way Dorle had never seen, stroking the soft recess at the base of the throat, where the skin was sunk between the collar bones.

"You'll know because it will fill you up inside."

● ● ●

"SWEETIE," SAYS THE WOMAN in the red shirt, "you got some strange notions, but I'm gonna get you through."

She grabs Dorle's hand and pulls her through the resurgent mass of summer tourists. She can see the enraged eyes of pedestrians parted by the woman's blunt drive. The second bus's doors sibilate in opening, and before she knows it, the woman's got her seated by a window in the front row. The bus driver, a lean, rangy, white-haired man, takes one look at the woman in the red shirt and decides not to ask them to move to the back. In some way, the scene reminds Dorle of the accident in Farewell: the cold, quiet lay of the street versus the hot, loud lights of the courtroom.

"Sometimes, you just gotta take control," the woman says.

Dorle notices drops of sweat on her upper lip, her hair frizzy at the ears.

"These people got no respect for the flag," the woman taps the graphic on her shirt. "Life, liberty, and the pursuit of happiness!"

The woman takes a deep breath.

"Freedom," she says more quietly. "Our freedom is everything."

● ● ●

THE PEARL EARRINGS WERE the beginning. Dorle learned how to fill herself up with things, with simple sensations of things, and if not the things themselves, then at least ideas of the things, those perfect forms that burned between dream and reality. The material world was a thick and hardened cornucopia one had to pry open.

Christmas was especially plentiful for prying. It was the one time of year her mother was home for more than a few days; Frau Wasser had neglected to take her daughter to the city as promised. All Dorle knew of her mother's life there was that she worked in a big bank downtown. She had started as a teller and had become a loan account manager, the only woman overseeing accounts in the whole building. That's why she wore fancy dresses, her father said. That's why it was hard for her to come home, because she had so many important clients to attend to. But Christmas was the exception. Frau Wasser not only returned home, but arrived bearing gifts: fruitcakes saturated in brandy; chocolates lined in glossy rows, some flat-topped and frilled with sugar stripes, which she could peel off with her fingernails, and others dense and lumpy with nuts; and hard peppermint candies, too, which she liked most of all because she could suck on them for hours, one after the other, never losing that zinging sweetness in her mouth. Frau Wasser also brought gift boxes, satin-red rectangles with silky green ringlets of ribbon, and she stacked them on the mantle above the fireplace. Dorle knew they wouldn't come down until a tree was placed in the living room and properly decorated.

When Dorle was eight, her father took her into the Sierra Nevada to find a tree. She recalls leaving the tiny town of Farewell, its collection of stucco wine estates and turn-of-the-century craftsman homes all clustered in the greenish golden hills at the head of a long, narrow, fertile valley. A large creek ran through the middle of town, in a tangle of briar and poison oak, and was bridged in several places—

"It's hopeless!" bursts the woman in the red shirt.

She's looking out the window at a group of Asian men and women who, in their spontaneous congregation, have blocked the pedestrian path that runs parallel to the bus route.

"I suppose they don't know any better," the woman says, as if being generous in her assessment.

Dorle scratches her face. Her allergies are getting worse, her skin itchy, encrusted. She pinches the bridge of her nose and throws her head back into the seat—

She was driving through Farwell with her father. Over the bridge and then left onto the highway. Turning right, she knew, would lead deep into the hills, where road and stream became one and plumbed the heart of a petrified forest. But they turned left, Herr Wasser steering the blue Chevy pickup out along the rim of the valley. The heater coughed warm air and made the vinyl bench seat smell like gloves. It was cool and humid, as winters always were in the valley, and the hilltops above were half-cloaked by fog. It took about an hour to reach the interstate, where the hills lulled, and the valley opened to the smoggy floodplains of the Sacramento.

"Can't tell from here, honey, but pretty soon you'll be seeing snow."

Snow. Dorle had seen it in movies. Large, fluffy flakes floating down on the lighted streets of America. Actors with arms outstretched as if the snow were something heaven-sent. She couldn't wait to see it. But first were the outskirts of a city. Blocks of buildings rigged like ships on the ocher floodplains. Gleams of tributaries and canals. The buildings grew larger and denser. There was a bridge over a wide section of water. She counted the seconds as the truck's tires hummed across it. Almost sixty. Then neighborhoods, more houses than Dorle had ever seen. Palm trees sticking out from wooden fences, ornamenting the dull sky.

"Is this where mommy lives?" she asked her father.

"Nope. This is Sacramento. Your mother spends her time in San Francisco."

His voice was flat while saying this.

"Don't worry about your mother. She's home now."

Dorle watched the land rumple into oak-laden hills, similar to the hills she knew in Farewell. Then the oaks turned into straighter, taller, pointier trees. They looked like skeletons with crooked, lint-clad limbs. They drove deeper into hills that were no longer hills but becoming something massive, foundational, platforming ranks upon ranks of the pointed trees. The pines marched through Dorle's mind like pikestaffs of a great army.

"You look worried, honey. It's dark like this in the foothills. But just wait. I know exactly where to find our tree."

Dorle began holding her breath around bends in the road, a new road that had veered left from the interstate. There were yellow signs with squiggly arrows. There was a river as twisted as the road itself, thickets splayed and frozen as if trampled by ice. Around the last bend, over the summit, the world opened forever.

"Now we can say we're in the mountains," Herr Wasser proclaimed.

She didn't know what she was looking at. She thought she had reached the clouds, broken through. What lay before her was a dreamland of wedding-dress white. The silk flowed on the body of the earth, tailored by the wind, in smooth fields fanning out and rumpled pleats where the fields met the forest, and even more delicate lacework along the river. She also saw a sun she had never seen before in a sky she had never seen before. Deep, deep blue sky. And a medallion of fire blazing through it, gilding the snow in blinding layers of gold. When she turned her head, she saw a castle of mountains rise up in the beating light. It was hard to tell if the peaks rested on the snow or on clouds; their base was pure, trackless white, their craggy battlements and towers crowned in blue ice.

"This is our kingdom," Herr Wasser said. "Down there, in the valley, we're commoners, growers of poison. Up here, we share the company of gods. Do you understand?"

Dorle nodded without understanding. They drove in silence, following the contours of sun-fired snow. Their eyes ached from the brightness. Her father reached over and removed a pair of sunglasses from the glove compartment.

"Put these on," he said.

The shades rose over her eyes and instantly cooled the world. Unaided, her father squinted against the light, fumbling over a half-remembered map in his mind. They came to a stop at an empty intersection. A run-down gas station stood kitty-corner. No customers. No attendants.

"I think we go left, toward the mountains," he said.

It scared her that he didn't know. Straight ahead were white meadows. Left was the pine forest. Fresh snow lay on the pointed treetops like crushed chalk.

"Yes, I'm almost sure now," he said.

They turned left into the forest. The road had been plowed into berms on both sides, frozen walls taller than the walls in their house. Sunlight erupted through the trees as the truck vroomed through the bobsled-like course, and Dorle's mind was dazzled each time the light broke through. Shade and sun pulsed in alternating rhythm against her temples, massaging her fears. She felt nearly dissolved when her father stopped the truck near a break in the berm and told her to lace up her boots.

It wasn't like the movies. The snow was wet and terrible. She cried trying to lift her own weight out of each footprint, each sunken hole, that her father had made before her. She was drowning in the snow, which seeped beneath her jacket and stung her skin. At one moment, she thought she lost her father, and the terror she felt was hot and sharp. Then he reappeared on her left side, swooping in like a film hero and hoisting her up on his shoulders. Her tearful eyes steamed against the cold and followed his outstretched arm to the point of his index finger. He was pointing at an angelic tree that hovered and hummed in the stillness of the forest. Its wood was as white as ivory. Its boughs were bristling green and tapered like a cone of wreaths.

"It's a white fir," he told her. "Our Christmas tree."

• • •

STAMER AND LI LOITER on the bridge, the river beneath them a cool magnet from which they don't want to break. Their conversation has turned to China's Cultural Revolution, Chairman Mao, and the Red Guard.

"If you look at the Chinese people now, you may think they're free," Li says. "In Beijing, the streets are full of riches. There's money. Fancy places to live. Fancy cars. People go to work in nice clothes and have big parties at night. They pretend to be like the Americans on TV, or the Europeans, the rich and the famous. But it's not real. Behind everything, they're watching you, making sure you don't question what you see. You can act like you're free, but if you try to do what you want, they come out and stop you. Very much like a play on stage. If you mess up what you're supposed to say, the man comes out from behind the curtain and grabs you."

Stamer looks down at a blank page in his journal. He snaps the book shut and slips it back into his pocket.

"I'd like to hike to the falls with you, Li, but I was wondering if we could wait for someone."

Li takes the straps hanging from his backpack and buckles them together around his waist. As he smooths the camera strap on his shoulder, his mouth curls into a curious smile. A sad smile. As if the gentle act of smiling were a relief from something inside.

"I never thought I would be here," he says. "Such a long way from where I started. Sure, I'll wait with you."

• • •

THOUSANDS OF LANTERNS FLOATED on the nighttime lake. Each flickering color was carried in a delicate paper box or cylinder. All the lanterns seemed to follow some invisible drift on the black water, forming the luminous spine of a dragon.

It was Li's eighth spring festival, and he was sitting on the shore with two classmates. The one on his right was a young girl named Danyu, to whom he had given the rest of his rice dumplings. She had silky black hair and dimples when she smiled. She wore glasses. Watching the colored lanterns play across her lenses, Li felt as if he were slipping into a parallel dimension, another world where the contents of his mind were unanchored, inverted, floating without prescription or limit. A single thought of loveliness alighted on Danyu's lips, which were like a carving in the dark flesh of a cherry tree. The puckered flesh thrilled his amorphous existence. Everything in his head and body was drawn toward those lips, as though life's purpose were suddenly as simple as a kiss.

"Have you heard of the city beneath the lake?" she asked.

Li shook his head, which was swirling with color.

"Beneath all the lakes in Beijing, there is a secret city. Only a few people know how to get there. The temples in Tianan are nothing compared to what's underground."

"I've never heard of this before," he said.

"You're not supposed to talk about it," said their other friend, who'd been throwing pebbles into the black water, watching them ripple the lantern light. "Everyone knows you're not supposed to talk about it."

"Is it where the Great Helmsman lives?" Li asked.

"No," said the boy. "The leaders don't even know about it. It was not built for them. There's only one way in. A secret door in the hutong."

As Li considered this, fireworks whistled and crackled across the sky—

"Who are we waiting for?" Li asks Stamer.

Stamer parries the question with another.

"Have you been up the Mist Trail before?"

"Never. Is it a woman you're waiting for?"

Surprised, Stamer locks his eyes onto his new friend's face, but it's as patient and kind as it's been all morning, perhaps a shade sadder, heavier.

Li answers himself:

"So much of what men do in this world is about a woman, isn't it?"—

Li had wandered into his father's study. On two walls perpendicular to each other stood dark, floor-to-ceiling bookcases. The rear case held titles of different heights and colors, different textures when Li pulled them out, one by one, and ran his hand over their covers. A few were stiff and bumpy like brail. Others were soft and smooth against his fingers.

The case on the sidewall was not the same. The books were uniform in profile, their bindings a grainy gold with red characters embossed on each spine. When Li reached up to pull one out, the book didn't budge. He tried another, but the books appeared to be fixed to the wall. He grew confused, tugging at the curious structure.

"Li!" his mother shouted.

Her hand whipped across his face. He remembers the stinging shock on his cheek, the sharp, rattling pain in his right eye as though the eyeball had been dislodged, then tears pouring from both eyes.

"Do not touch! I told you not to come in here!"

He was crying, trying to explain he just wanted a book. He pointed to the sidewall and muttered how the books were stuck together like bricks.

She grabbed his hand.

"That is not for you to question," she said in a firm, instructive tone. "You must accept reality. Looking deeper will only lead to trouble."

She was taller than his father, ferocious when tested but otherwise silent and stealthy.

That same night, she snuck up on him again while he was doing his home studies. His mind had drifted, and he'd set his pencil burning in the corners of the worksheet, drawing circles and stars, dragons with tongues of fire, trees that grew into mountaintops, flowers with petals like the beaks of birds.

Without warning, his mother struck his hand: "You'll have no future unless you learn to focus. It is a poor man who doesn't have pride to succeed."

She found scissors in a nearby drawer and made him cut off the corners of all the sheets in his workbook and also any free space in the margins that could entice him. His drawings fell to the floor in clipped shards and long, curling strips. Once, when she turned around, he reached down to pick up an eye he'd drawn—a dark oval fissure in the paper, a stark, unstitched opening into some new, wondrous world— but she was quickly upon him, his hand wincing from a blow so fast and precise he hadn't seen it.

He tried to comfort his hand with the other, but she grabbed his wrist:

"You must learn to tolerate pain," she said. "It is necessary."

He nodded. He'd already learned how not to cry in front of her.

• • •

"My father worked for the Chinese government. He was an intelligence officer, a spy on his own people, and my mother was his greatest protector."

Stamer's unnerved. He imagines a series of paintings hanging on the walls of a long hallway. Thick oil portraits of emperors succeeding one another, all the faces pudgy and imperious except the last one. The eyes of the last emperor have been removed, and someone is standing behind the wall looking through the dead emperor's eyes, watching everyone who passes through the corridor. The image is simultaneously absurd and menacing.

"I...I'm sorry," Stamer stutters. "I...I should have told you my plans. I...I met a woman this morning. She's the one I'm waiting for."

Li notes his friend's stutter and ponders the invisible power of the state, a perceived power, to compel confession of forbidden love, even in the mountains.

"Does she know you're waiting for her?"

Stamer shakes his head.

"She was actually upset with me. She was trying to give a deer some water, and I told 'er it wasn't a good idea."

"So she doesn't know you're waiting for her, and she doesn't like you?"

"Yeah, it's dumb. It's been a while since I've felt attracted to someone like that."

"What does it feel like?"

Stamer makes a weird, muffled sound, a low but uneven vibration against the roof of his mouth.

"It feels like waking up, I guess. It feels like the world's pulling you to your feet, and your body's burning."

"What did you do before you came here? You said you worked in Las Vegas?"

"Nice try," Stamer says. "If you're trying to change the conversation, I want to hear about your father before anything else. A spy, huh?"

Li loosens the straps on his pack and sits on the parapet over the river. He pats the camera dangling from one shoulder, as if it were a pet, and then takes off his glasses and wipes the lenses with the underside of his T-shirt.

"Well, we have some time. You're sure this woman is coming here?"

Stamer shrugs.

"I believe so."

Li ponders the rich, blue air in front of him. Its beauty bothers him.

"It seems you won't tell me about Vegas. I have seen the commercials. What happens in Vegas stays in Vegas. I get it. But I don't want to talk about my father. I'm like you. I had a hard father who worked against me. It's too much to think about."

Stamer also fidgets with his pack, boots, shorts, belt, hat. He sits on the ledge beside Li, the water below rushing in their ears the same way the breeze above rushes through the trees.

"The artist is the only person who can control the world," Li says.

"I don't understand."

"Early on I knew I was an artist. I had the artist's eye. I could see things, details, no one else could see. I could see every little fact of the world like they were pieces of a puzzle. Everywhere. In my house. In my room. A little crack in the wall. But I could never put the pieces together. I'd try harder—just like my mother wished—study harder, dress better, act more important than I was. I'd try to control everything, every detail, until it made me sick with pain and I lost it all."

"Sorry about before when I thought you were an engineer."

Li smiles differently this time, his lips drawn up in a half-smirk, a clever pouch.

His smiles change like the light, Stamer thinks. *Like the light I saw dancing on the water.*

"I was training to become an engineer before studying art," Li says. "Just to please my parents. But I never stopped drawing. I learned

I could control the world on paper. I had this energy inside me that wanted to get out and grab everything."

He waves his hand through the air, like a rudder cutting water to find new direction.

"It just built up more and more, this energy. My parents tried to control me. But the more they made me sit and study math and science, the worse it got. I'd run through the streets to get rid of it. It was like I was on fire. If I kept still for too long, it would burn a hole through me. I had to release it, or else I'd die. I learned later how to release it when I went to university. It was the only way I ever felt control. Control and freedom at the same time."

Stamer leans back on his elbows and lets his head loll in the sunlight.

"When I was young, I drew in secret," Li continues. "I used anything I could get. Ink. Chalk. Charcoal sometimes. My drawings got better, but I had to keep them hidden. If my mother found them, I was punished. It went on like this for years—until the test."

Li searches Stamer's face for comprehension.

"In China, if you're not a well-connected boy, you must take a test before going to college. This test is administered by the government, and it decides your future as an adult. It is everything. Some don't take it; some go to the factories. The ones with *guanxi*—connections—get into the good schools no matter what. They get the good jobs.

"I grew up in Beijing in a poor family. You may think I was connected because my father was a spy, but you're not realizing how many spies the Chinese government puts to work. We weren't special. I had to take the test, and I had to do well. I knew I wanted to be an artist, but I also knew as I got older it was not a choice for me at the time. Artists were looked down upon. It's different now. There are world-famous artists like Ai Weiwei. You'd think it's Paris now, with all the new galleries and dealers, but it was different when I started out. You either worked in the factories or you managed the people working in the factories. Your occupation was determined by the test. So I stopped drawing for a while and studied hard as my mother wished. And I did very well on the test. I got into Peking University."

"In a way, an engineer is an artist," Stamer says. "You're building something."

Li frowns. The depressive expression distorts the delicate features of his face.

"That's where you're wrong. Creativity is not valued by the Chinese government. We do what we're told; we imitate. Designs are borrowed, bought, or stolen. The information is hacked, or someone is bribed. Where I apprenticed my first year of college, we used to call these kinds of researchers 'ducks,' because they were fed the best food during the day, made fat and happy, but roasted as soon as their work was done."

Li laughs.

"Not really roasted but disposed of. You see, the Party would never allow you to create something on your own. Because then you would become more powerful than them."

Li looks down on the river, fluting through a city of stones, and he sees the streets of Beijing. He sees the hutong, the ancient alleyways, and in the very center of the labyrinth a gray brick wall with a single red door as bright and fiery as love.

"When I came to the park this morning, the first thing I thought was that no one could imitate this. No one could steal this."

● ● ●

Have you ever been to jail? Have you felt the concrete floor through your socks? Taken your meals from a plastic tray that smells like rubber? Have you gotten up at midnight to vomit in a metal toilet? Ever heard the sound of a bunch of women crying in the dark? You know nothing of America.

Dorle is staring at the large woman in the red shirt, who is sitting on a bench near the concession stand. They'd gotten off the bus together, the last stop before the bridge, but the woman hadn't said a word about where she was going. Now she's devouring a corn dog, the American flag graphic on her shirt cracking, peeling.

"Sweetie, you're gonna need some protein for the hike," she says.

Minutes before Dorle was standing in line, eyes searching the menu for diet soda, when the woman in red began bantering with the cashier in a way that embarrassed her. It was not what the woman was saying, but her gruff inflection, her domineering body language.

Now Dorle's considering how to disengage herself from their curious alliance.

A clean break is the best way.

The same thing her ex-husband told her when she was released on parole.

Dora and I just need a fresh start.

It wasn't my fault, she whispers to herself. To the judge's shiny pink head.

Chester Winfield is dead.

He was jaywalking at night. I couldn't see him in the headlights, Your Honor.

You've already pled guilty to the charges, Ms. Wasser.

It wasn't my fault. She remembers how the words slipped from her mouth like water. The reporter from the paper wrote them down and bannered them in a headline the next day. Her slip became the mainstream. An accident, an aberration, became the definitive norm. To all minds but her own, Dorle Wasser was remorseless.

"A clean break is the best way," she tells the woman in the red shirt.

She's up on her feet tearing at the road with deadly stride. She's popping her ears on purpose to block any protest. She's patting herself down to make sure she didn't leave anything behind. Fanny pack. Water bottle. She spots the bridge ahead, where some people have gathered on the edge over the water.

Fuck you! You don't know me! How dare you judge me! What gives you the right? She is my child!

The water's white then clear, white then clear, a cool, constant absolution. She imagines standing beneath the trees, scrubbing her bones with the snowmelt—

Not like the way she washes Dora with a soapy sponge, softly, exultingly, before lifting her to the showerhead. The hot water hisses. Dora, eighteen months old, cries in fear, but Dorle props her on her hip and swings sideways so she can see the water falling on her breast, dripping from her nipples. Dorle uses her finger to smooth the flecks on her chest. The flattened water looks like melted pearls. No longer afraid, Dora reaches out and opens her hand. The shower streams tickle her upturned palm, and she smiles in wonder, her mouth a toothy question mark. The growing steam plumes Dorle's head and leaves a hot tang of iron in both their mouths. Dorle lifts her daughter back up to the showerhead, and this time Dora shrieks in joy. She shrieks, then licks the beads of water on her lips. For a moment, in that slippery embrace, mother and daughter are fluid as one—

Dorle wipes her eyes as she walks, smelling baby shampoo, scented like lavender, and the cloying aroma of a new diaper, the mixture of baby powder and rash cream, and Dora's sweet saliva pooling between her pink gums and lower lip, trickling down her chin.

Dorle's heart skips when she sees the familiar man sitting on the bridge's parapet. Stamer, momentarily entranced by the water, looks up and grins. Dorle puts her head down, wrenches her hat against her skull. She tries to make it past.

"Li! Here she is."

His voice catches her attention like a hook. She stops and glares at him defiantly. Then she notices the Chinese man sitting next to him. Something about his face, almost guileless, almost angelic, softens her hostility.

"I was hoping to see you again," Stamer says. He's about to say they've been waiting for her but catches himself. "I wanted to apologize for this morning. I didn't mean to offend you. I was concerned was all."

"Well—" Dorle begins.

She's searching for a phrase to match the strange, spontaneous flood of affection inside her.

"It's water under the bridge, I guess."

Li laughs, rising to his feet. Stamer jumps up and steps in front of him.

"This is Li. He's from China. We're going up the Mist Trail together. Want to join us?"

To the judge's shiny pink head. To the polished desks and benches of the courtroom. She remembers how, when the sentence was read, each word shot her heart. Six years in prison with the possibility of parole after twelve months. Twenty-nine days in jail counted toward time served. *Bailiff, please take the defendant into custody.* When she felt the manacles cutting into her wrists for the second time in her life, she was absolutely convinced she would never again be normal in the company of other people.

"I'm going to Vernal Falls," she tells the two men. "I can't stop you if you're going the same way."

PART TWO

S tamer had an imaginary friend until he left home. Sparky stayed with him in his adolescence. A disembodied voice. A shade-crossed spot of light. His friend appeared and disappeared and reappeared like the wind that animated the forest fringes above his hometown. He never told anyone about it. He was afraid they'd laugh at him. The phenomenon was private, sacred. It was the part of his brother he had kept alive. There were times, in his mind, when Sparky became Kristopher and vice versa. The two identities ran together like a stream, their attributes blended in one mystic presence. Stamer's attention alone could invoke the spirit, which spoke to him in times of trial, loneliness, reproach, whenever he strayed from what his father had taught him. In this way, Sparky was his confidante, his conscience, the deepest reference point within himself—a buried mirror.

The voice faded, though, when he left for home, partly because he'd replaced it with the voice of a young woman, a fleshy face full of light.

Kimberly Trenton was the daughter of an industrialist. She had a smart, narrow face, with sinuous lips, and a jagged chin that slanted to the left when she spoke. She was built of smooth, supple limbs, like a maple tree, and had naturally pale skin that browned beautifully in the summer sun of their last year together in Prideport.

He'd fallen in love with her a week before graduation, a hazy Sunday afternoon outside his father's church. They walked to the riverbank while talking about the future. He was planning to head west to Denver, to attend a religious-based business school where the pastor had several personal connections. His grades were not great, but they were not terrible, and all the times he'd set up chairs for the Fellowship of the Christ youth group somehow counted as extracurricular activity and community service. She was planning to attend Brown University, to study biology and eventually become a doctor. Her father also had connections, but her grades were far better than his. She was naturally intelligent, unusually mature for her age, and possessed a precocious understanding of the human body. She made him nervous.

"I ja…just want to leave town," he stammered. "S…see what's out there."

She smiled at his stuttering. Her lips were slippery and soft-looking, he remembers.

"I'm like you," she said. "I don't ever want to come back here."

That night, they both snuck out and met at the river. She laid him down at the edge of a grassy inlet, water gurgling in the bulrush shallows, and she gave him head. It was the first time someone touched him intimately, besides himself, and he bucked wildly as he came in her mouth. It felt like stars exploding in his head, down his spine, then just the cool night sky, strangely pure and guiltless.

The times he had satisfied himself always left a stain of guilt. The pastor had taught him that his body was a temple to be kept immaculate as an offering to God. Only purity, free from the stain of sin, could enter the Kingdom of Heaven. Masturbation was a sin, the pastor had warned. Thus, before meeting Kimberly, every time Stamer had worked his own flesh into shimmering strings of pearls, he was overcome by shame. Sitting in the pews of his father's church, he would feel unclean and conniving. The guilt would make stones of his eyes, sinking toward the brilliant immolations the pastor made of candles. Yet left by himself, days later, even hours later, the urge would invariably return. It would overpower the guilt, and again he'd live exalted in those few hard stroking seconds, exquisite seconds, before producing the shameful pearls, quivering in his hands.

But Kimberly destroyed the cycle altogether. The urge was there, but never the remorse. They made a midnight habit of meeting at the river, lying down in the cool grass, and exploring each other's bodies. Ecstasy was their mutual goal: sensation beyond sin. By their third night, she had taken his virginity. There was no feeling of guilt or ruin, just a smoldering, hungering glory. He knew that he was in love with her. And this love obliterated the flimsy structures of his faith. He grew strong like fire. His eyes burned bright at all hours of the day. He began to speak with the power of his love, with its fluency, and soon lost the stutter that had given rise to his nickname.

The pastor guessed what was happening, and one night confronted Stamer by the door just as he was slipping out.

"Remember, my son," he said in a voice wasted and hoarse, his age-eaten face ghostly in the moon-shadows. "Satan first planted sin in the heart of a woman. Don't jeopardize your future by giving into temptation."

Stamer opened the door and left, carrying with him the silent, pained expression on his father's face, the head descending in shame.

Later, sitting on the riverbank, he told Kimberly what had happened.

"Of course he'd say that," she said. "I don't wanna be the one to tell you if you don't know, but your father's been fucking another woman."

The summer night sky tilted. Stamer's head fell to the water's edge, where river and sky became indistinguishable, stars scattered randomly.

"You're a liar," he said, sitting back up. "My father's never cheated on my mother."

"He has—he still is—with that Evelyn woman from church. You know, she's tall, big boobs, wears shoulder pads."

Stamer knew the woman. Blonde hair fried by a curling iron. Big teeth smeared with lipstick. She wore tight dresses that made frictional noises when she walked. She'd been over to his house once for Bible study. He now remembered his mother had sat silently at the kitchen counter reading a magazine, while his father, the woman, and the rest of the participants had sat in the living room reciting scripture.

"I don't believe you. Why would you think that?"

"Stamer, I'm sorry," she said with an air of reconciliation. "Everybody in Prideport knows about it. Why do you think your mom stays home all the time?"

He recalled his mother's face during Kristopher's memorial service all those years before. A proud face wracked by indignity.

He turned toward Kimberly. They made fierce love on the cool grass, which was heading out in spikes of seed.

• • •

STAMER GLANCES AT DORLE as they start up the Mist Trail. At first, she hikes with a straight and confident step, but then she wanders off-balance, veering from side to side as though avoiding some invisible obstacle in the middle of the trail. Slowly she regains composure and resumes a straightforward direction, but does so with an overdetermined springiness in her stride, almost a skip, suggesting she, too, at some level, is conscious of her own imbalanced state.

Her overcompensation, her vulnerability, inexplicably fuels Stamer's desire. He imagines undressing her in a sun-warmed meadow beside a snow-swollen stream. She resists, fusses, then surrenders with a whimper.

Sweat drips from his forehead, stings his eyes, salts the fantasy.

• • •

STAMER ANTICIPATED IN THE season's change the end of his romance with Kimberly. Before they'd become involved, she'd broken up with her longtime high school boyfriend. It was clear she was preparing for a new life in the Ivy Leagues and that his window with her would widen or narrow with the summer sun.

The first chill of fall signaled her departure. Dressing themselves after their last meeting beside the river, she had little to say.

"We had fun, didn't we?"

She laughed. But her moonlit face, in the seconds already parting them, took on seriousness, a coldness that wrenched his heart.

He nodded.

"We'll always remember this," she said, "our little place down by the river."

The leaves of the maple trees were just yellowing when Stamer left for Denver. The year was 1978. He was driving a primer-gray Ford pickup he'd bought from a pumpkin farmer in Prideport. He'd earned the money while working for the pastor, organizing youth groups and Bible camps, sometimes just babysitting young parishioners. Though he and his father worked together all summer, a discernible silence grew between them. For his part, Stamer had let the silence grow. He wasn't mad at his father, but he was sad for his mother, who would now be alone. And he was sad for himself, for his new awareness of the shame that followed him and his family. He began sensing looks and whispers and gestures in the grocery store, the movie theater, the rolling rink. Whether they were born of contempt or compassion, whether they were even real, he didn't know. But he knew his father had made no attempt to broach the subject or bridge the silence. He knew his father knew that he knew. The sin had stained all.

Stamer's estrangement from his family was not his primary pain, however. He was still mourning the loss of Kimberly when he finally left town. There were hugs and goodbyes, his mother's tears, his father's tepid encouragement, but they felt superficial compared to the deep sense of loss within him. Driving through eastern Pennsylvania, he realized he hadn't put up a fight. He hadn't even offered an alternative. He had simply accepted his fate. He had accepted that Kimberly was better than him, that she had access to wealth and prestige and a superior lifestyle. He'd let her believe the same. He'd resigned his heart, his pride, and now the loss, the bereavement, the sense of injustice, the resentment, all spread through his being as a leaden malaise.

"You learned something important," Sparky said to him while crossing into Ohio, his friend now a pale glimmer in the rearview mirror. "Everything you love can disappear."

Stamer stared through the windshield, the road unraveling under his motion, all the knotty space ahead harshly revealed in the sunlight. Dwarf hills. Coils of tree.

"Wha…wha…" he began to stutter.

Then he clenched his mouth. He exhaled through his nostrils like a bull. He would force himself not to stutter.

"I don't want to talk to you anymore. I don't want to think about it anymore. I want to find something new."

That was the last time he openly talked to Sparky. When the freeway unfolded across the Great Plains, like a bridge across a sea of corn, the openness uprooted tears from his eyes. In that revelation of flatness, he thought he would see his brother hanging above the cornrows like a scarecrow. But he didn't. There was no ghost following him. By the time he reached Denver, he'd already decided to keep going. He stayed one night in a ramshackle hotel on the edge of the plains. He twisted and moaned in his sleep. He dreamed of Kimberly's moonlit face in the reeds. Of Kristopher's skeleton in a burrow pit, of wind-bent grass. In the morning, he set out for the mountains.

● ● ●

"I NEED A BREAK," Dorle says, rolling her shoulders.

The three of them stop at a bend in the trail. To their right, the canyon drops steeply into a lush thicket, like a blanket conforming to the boulders along the river. The sound of mountain water is a steady rushing sound, underscoring the scattered calls of birds. Nuthatches, chickadees, somewhere the beating wings of a hummingbird. And deeper within the forest, in a small, shadowed hollow, the wild, sharp, quavering song of a hermit thrush.

To their left, the canyon wall lifts steeply. Lumpy outcrops of granite half-buried in leafy mats of soil. The pale and coarse outcrops sparkle in the sunlight. At the foot of the slope, adjacent to the trail, sits a stone basin brimming with spring water.

"Look at this," Li says, approaching the basin with the curiosity of a geologist.

He kneels down beside the stone and ripples the water with his hand. He takes off his backpack, revealing a dark stamp of sweat on his shirt, and finds the plastic reservoir inside. It hangs from the pack like a vulcanized organ. He detaches the bladder from the hose and then sinks it into the spring water, bubbling around his hands.

"Careful," Stamer warns. "Giardia."

"I've not heard this term," Li says.

"Diarrhea," Stamer points to the water.

"Oh, stop it!" Dorle says, slapping Stamer across the chest.

It's the first time she's touched him, and the impact jolts him, thrills him, like an electric shock.

"Don't listen to him. You'll be fine," she tells Li. "He was giving me grief this morning because I was trying to give some poor little deer a sip of water."

Stamer sees her face is flushed pink, her blue eyes now beaming, her dainty lips open in playfulness. He can't resist a smile of his own.

"Listen," he teases, "that little deer of yours was a buck. I guess you could say I saved your life."

"Oh, God," she says. "Let the man have his water."

Li lifts the bladder and takes a few gulps from the opening before refastening it to his pack. He stands and licks his lips triumphantly. He looks at them, from one to the other, with amused knowing.

"The water's good. I've heard this expression in Los Angeles. People say, 'Get a room.'"

His grin sharpens.

"You two should get a room. Or a tent."

Stamer snorts as he turns back to the trail, but not before seeing Dorle's face turn from pink to a deep shade of scarlet.

• • •

WHEN STAMER DROVE INTO the Rocky Mountains at the age of eighteen, he discovered the light he had once chased through the forest. It lay on the high peaks like a recumbent thought, strained of all effort, pure and plotless and golden, slipping down cliffsides, dripping into shadowy cirques where remnant snows still bled trickles of water. On the shoulders of the peaks, which were ribboned with yellow quaking aspen and dark green timber, the light achieved a clarity as deep and still as he had ever seen, as though the light had limitless range and power to hold everything in place, every object, every thought, every feeling, every single attribute of the world.

He pulled off the pass and got out of his truck. The second the door shut, a great wind sang in his ears. The zesty smell of decaying wildflowers filled his nose. He realized he would never return east. The West, all its wild light, was his new mistress.

He drove through the night. Up and down lonesome roads, empty valleys, curving canyons, bursts of starlight at every summit. He had his windows down to smell the autumnal grasses, the late, dying flowers, the dark, redolent pines that tore past his vision. He wanted to keep going, to keep driving all the way to the Pacific, to his radiant blue dream of the Pacific, but finally, unable to ignore his own exhaustion, he landed like a wind-whipped leaf on a dingy motel in the outskirts of Salt Lake City.

Stamer's first impression of the city was that it was minute and delicate against the mountains. In high school, he'd made trips to Pittsburgh, New Jersey, and New York, where the buildings dominated the landscape, what was left of the landscape. The cities in the East were piled heedlessly, entrenched, redoubled in their structures. Industry replaced the soil, girded the bedrock. The few skyscrapers now before him seemed flimsy in contrast, toylike against the huge, shark-toothed ramparts of the Wasatch Front.

In the scruffy suburbs surrounding the city—oak-choked grids steepled with Mormon churches—he found a used car lot and sold his truck. He pocketed the cash and hitchhiked downtown. At the first bank he found, he applied for a teller position, citing his experience managing his father's accounts. That same day, he was assigned to a vacant register at the very last window.

Squeals & Anderson Security resided in a historic, thirteen-story mid-rise. The granite for the building's stately walls had been quarried in Little Cottonwood Canyon southeast of the city. The bank's founders had gone to great lengths to showcase their frontier history, commissioning sculptures of Indian faces and buffalo horns for the building's classical friezes and cornices. Inside, in the vast vaulted lobby, stretched murals of the western landscape, all open and pink, with lone horse-drawn carriages riding along the horizon. The panoramas were offset by huge still-life portraits of dusty padlocked safes.

Stamer's cash register was an antique model. Iron keys. Brass trimmings. The manager showed him which key opened the cash drawer.

"Try it. It's yours now," he said.

At the touch of the restive iron, creaking down, the enormous drawer sprang into Stamer's mind. It sprang out and a golden bell rang in his ears. The conflated smells of coins and paper money drifted on the air, whetting his appetite. He'd forgotten his own hunger, and now, oddly thinking of his father's sin, he was charged with desire. Money, food, sex, light—he was starving.

"Why don't you go wash up in the men's room and wrap up the day with us," the manager said. "I have an extra suit in my office."

Stamer looked down and realized he hadn't changed his clothes since leaving Pennsylvania. He was in blue jeans and a green flannel shirt. Pressing his chin down, he snuck a smell of his own body odor. It smelled of Indian summer sweat, a pungent musk, but also of dried grass, broken flowers, dirt, asphalt, exhaust. Everything along the road, the journey. Sensing eyes still upon him, he sniffed again, and he was ashamed.

• • •

STAMER'S SWEATING NOW. THE asphalt trail steepens in the sunlight, and the pleasant oak-shade of the hillside gives way to sunbaked, crumbling granitic grains. It's finally getting hot, he thinks. He smells himself without bending his head. He hasn't bathed for days, and he hopes the breeze is blowing south so Dorle doesn't smell him. He's ashamed of the smell.

The dry stretch of trail reminds Stamer of the Nevada desert and the money in his tent down in the valley. It reminds him of his own desiccated spirit, the dried depth of it, the hardened lines of fate like lines in an aging face.

He pictures Forster's face. Forster was his best friend in adulthood. He had a pinkish, snickering face, weasel-like, and two cross-hatches of sandy-blond hair. There was a moment, Stamer remembers, when the features of the face turned stern and proud and the brown beady eyes opened in sadness. *Less than all cannot satisfy man.*

It was something Forster always said, a quote from William Blake. He was obsessed with the Romantics.

Now Stamer feels his eyes tighten as a wave of yearning rises and falls within.

• • •

BY THE END OF his first week at Squeals & Anderson, Stamer had become addicted to the smells and sounds of money. Minted currency was an object he could hold. It was an object that he could control, that would stay where he put it, and which maintained blind and cold allegiance to his desires. Its social value in the society around him provided even greater control. He could move materials according to his whims, stock his favorite possessions, and someday, all plans abiding, purchase a home near the mountaintops he'd fallen in love with.

Near the end of his first month at the bank, he'd made enough money for a deposit on a roomy, bay-windowed suite a few blocks from Temple Square. In the following months, he purchased the finest clothes and furniture he could afford, a used television set, a cassette stereo system, and a random assortment of wall-ready art. At the same time he was building his material wealth, he was reading every book he could on banking and finance, economics and philosophy. He developed a deep regard for the work of Ayn Rand, and with her tenets systematically replaced the religious values he'd inherited as a child. He fashioned himself a capitalist, grounded in rational self-interest, and was eager to share his borrowed theories with his coworkers, making it a point of pride that he'd effectively skipped college but was nonetheless wiser.

During the week, he walked to work beside the old stone buildings that were being slowly subsumed by glass and steel skyscrapers. He lunched at nearby restaurants recommended by his manager and others. An overpriced bar and grill. An overpriced deli. A cheaper Tibetan eatery in the Avenues. Soon enough, in the revolving lunch hours of the domino-like days, he found them. He joined them. Not just his manager, but several account managers, department heads, and corporate officers. They were men of a certain cut and aspect. Pressed suits. Polished shoes. Handsome faces and controlled demeanors. Confident words and gestures. He became their protégé. They told him they sensed their own greatness in him, for he was young, intelligent, personable, and ambitious. Whenever he was alone, he imagined they all talked about him; they would laud his street smarts, his book smarts, his relentless drive. *That guy will leave his mark on the world.*

Their affections, however, seemed to wane in the winter months. There were fewer lunches together. The office, and the city itself, hibernated under a permanent blanket of snow. The men he still managed to meet seemed stuffy and stolid in the cold. Thus Stamer slowly retreated into himself, read more and more.

In the winter evenings, he'd stroll beneath the fairy-bright Christ-mas lights of Temple Square. He found the Mormon girls touring the lights unbelievably beautiful. They were like rare winter birds with blonde plumage trailing from woolen hats. They had glossy smiles, hot and wild in the freezing air. Yet he remained aloof, not exactly afraid of them, but unsure how to proceed. His desire was there, as fierce as ever, but its execution was lost in a greater sense of estrangement. He kept recalling his nights with Kimberly. The memories seeped into his consciousness like firelight from the other side of the mountains, all the way across the snowy plains, there, buried in the frozen forests of his youth, icicles tinkling against the remembered heat. Whenever he thought he'd exorcised those old loves, the ghost of Kimberly, the face of his father, or the voice of Kristopher would stab him sharper than before. But he wouldn't give in. He wouldn't call or write. He wouldn't return whatever affection was sent his way across the continent. Instead he found new ways to organize his cash—a silver clip in his pocket, a fireproof safe in his closet. At work, he was devastated to learn senior members of the bank had formed a ski club without him. There had been no invitation, despite prior luncheons, and he realized how unini-tiated he remained among the ranks. After learning of a lavish New Year's Eve Party in Park City, to which he was also not invited, he refo-cused on his work, furious with purpose, and converted his feelings of alienation and inferiority into a powerful show of customer service, into a thundering smile and lightning-bolt handshake. As the winter's exclusion thawed into spring, his superiors' attentions returned.

Near the end of his first year, they made him a loan officer. He left his beloved cash register for a cubicle maze on the second floor. He was equipped with a filing cabinet, an adding machine, and a chrome stapler. These and other office implements hummed with productiv-ity as he worked through the days. He focused on his arithmetic and documentation the way a composer focuses on each note, each lift. Literally he hummed when riffling through customers' financials. He joked and laughed with prospective debtors, both in person and on the phone. If their credit was sound, he shook their hands, faxed them the documents, signed a thousand dotted lines. If their credit was poor, he ended the conversation as quickly as possible. Within two quarters, he'd developed one of the most profitable debt portfolios on the entire mortgage floor.

"Will you tell me your secret?" his new manager asked one afternoon.

The manager was an excitable kind of man, with a snub nose and glasses. He didn't have Stamer's cool charm. He didn't have Stamer's thick brown hair and Romanesque nose or his small gray eyes that stared through people so sure and keen.

"Cars," Stamer told him. "I used to drive an old Ford truck. Now I drive a new Thunderbird. I look at their cars, sir. Well, I can see what kind of loans they have on their cars then see the year and model. If they have nice cars, I assume they're moving up in the world and will make their loan payments. If they have poor cars, or no cars, I politely tell them to try another bank."

This revelation spread through the echelons of upper management. Soon Stamer was invited not only to lunches but dinner parties. On Friday nights, he'd dress in his best casual wear and saunter up the hills behind the capitol building to one of many extravagant homes. Some of his superiors belonged to the Mormon faith, and they offered soft drinks in lieu of cocktails during their gatherings. Others, usually the younger associates, made a point of offering the finest, most expensive spirits they could get at the state liquor store.

One of the latter was a man named Forster Cutting, a well-known socialite in the non-Mormon circles. He didn't work for the bank directly but was an investment consultant for a number of businesses and organizations, including Squeals & Anderson. He lived at the top of Memory Grove Park in a three-story hillside condo that had a jutting balcony. Forster happened to be standing on the balcony the balmy spring night Stamer came walking up to the party. He could see the solitary figure against the lighted windows of the second floor, where numerous faces mingled into dark splotches on the inside glass.

"Hello down there," the man called.

Stamer stopped below, looking up toward the dashing promontory of a face that caught city light in a superficial net of sweat. The collar of an open silk shirt hung rakish in the dark like the frond of an exotic palm, like a dark slippery tongue sabotaging the institutional moralism that had built the city.

"I hope I have the right place. I'm looking for Forster Cutting."

"You have the right place," Forster said. "Less than all cannot satisfy man."

"What?"

"Less than all cannot satisfy man. Blake."

"Who?"

A throaty laugh rocketed in the surrounding trees.

"Come in," Forster said. "You must be from the bank."

The condo's first floor was cluttered and dim. Stamer could make out heaps of clothes, scattered books, and sealed boxes stacked in the corners. Traveling up a carpeted staircase, the space turned on some bright, dazzling axis of life to reveal the party in full swing on the second floor. There were women in short, slanting dresses, strewn with glitter, their naked legs roving, and men in sport jackets, unbuttoned silk shirts, with thickly moussed hair and giant, laughing white teeth. The clinking of cocktail glasses and champagne flutes traveled across the room like a glissando of chimes. On the pinkish walls, in white washes of recessed lights, hung multitudes of paintings—so many that their frames touched. Stamer walked to the center painting as soft rock music spilled from a nearby stereo. From all the paintings the centerpiece beckoned him. It was of a woman painted in rich oils. Dark hair, brown skin, silvery eyes. Lips red like a fresh wound. Stamer was drawn to her, blinked, before realizing it was merely a face, no body, blazing from a lashed background of dark green and purple.

"The tiger," said a man who'd crept up behind him.

Stamer turned to find Forster's dashing face softened in the interior light. The eyes were an ordinary brown, the hair a sandy shade of blond. He thought the man could be no more than five years older than himself.

"Mr. Cutting, sorry, I was admiring this painting."

"Please, Forster's my name. I might drop my last name altogether. It would take a little paperwork but would be worth it, wouldn't it?"

"To change your name?"

"To be like the forest," he pointed toward the painting, "where the tiger burns so bright."

Stamer froze.

"My goodness, man, you need some instruction in the art of Romanticism. Come have a drink with me on the terrace."

Forster plucked a tumbler from a mahogany hutch on the perpendicular wall. In the upper compartments stood wooden masks of a lighter stain. A fanged fiend. A flat, frowning face. The man poured red wine weeping along the sides of the tumbler then reached for an open bottle of Coca-Cola.

"Kalimotxo," he said. "Red wine and Coke. The Basques of Nevada drink this. But you're curious about the masks. They're from my travels in the isles."

Stamer took the glass and sipped the mixture. It was syrupy-sweet then acrid in his mouth, working upon his brain almost instantly.

"Which islands?"

"The Happy Isles," Forster grinned. "Men can only dream of such places. Follow me back outside, will you?"

On the balcony, the night was cool and quiet. At the bottom of the canyon, the starry fortress of the Mormon temple glowed in a wash of aquamarine light, as if the light were upwelling from a hidden spring beneath the city, flowing in luminous curtains over the clean stone faces, suspending the structure in a permanent state of exaltation. The other buildings of downtown Salt Lake City drifted on the dark earth behind, their checkered lights like the manifestation of some wild, entropic destiny.

"Without that, the whole thing falls apart," Forster said.

"Without what?"

"The temple. The covenant."

Stamer sipped the concoction; it spiraled into his stomach.

"The covenant?"

Forster pulled a cigar from his shirt, a chrome lighter from his pants. The click of the lighter's lid opening and then flicks of the flint wheel inside all reminded Stamer of the dainty sounds of money. A small flame whooshed in the night. Spicy smoke billowing through the air.

"The belief, my friend, that God and mankind have reached an agreement. That temple represents the covenant. As long as men do their part, God will provide."

"Do you believe that?"

Forster laughed.

"Of course. Don't you?"

Stamer couldn't read his new friend's face in the darkness.

"I don't believe in God," he proclaimed.

Forster laughed even louder, beyond the cool realm of irony.

"Of course you do. You just don't know it. 'Less than all cannot satisfy man.' The wisest thing a poet ever wrote, don't you think?"

"You're telling me that without that down there, none of this would work, that there wouldn't be a place for men like us who work with money and finance enterprise, that science and art and culture wouldn't exist?"

"That's exactly what I'm telling you. Out of curiosity, which do you believe comes first, science, art, or culture? No, no, I don't believe in the finer points of Mormonism or Catholicism or Judaism or Buddhism. I don't accept the rituals of any religion. But I know their covenant with God, however carved out, binds the world together."

Stamer took another swig. The alcohol was unraveling his mind. He felt as if he were dreaming the whole scene. The balcony in the trees. Whispers and sighs from other balconies in stranger trees. City lights below twinkling on the plum-sweet, purple air. On the other side of the windows flashed a tall, dark-haired beauty in a denim jacket over a black dress. For a moment she stood in profile against the glass, her painted lips as soft and pouty as the petals of a black rose.

"You don't look like someone who's religious," Stamer said.

"You're misunderstanding me. We're all religious about one thing or another. I take people's money and turn it into large fortunes. My religion is based on the covenant between man and investor. My clients worship at my altar, endow me with superhuman powers to make them wealthy. As long as I provide, they don't question our relationship. They assume the world is just and prosperous, and it is—precisely because they're willing to believe it is. The world doesn't run on useless facts. There'll be nothing left when the naysayers have torn down all our idols. Believing is everything. Less. Than. All. Cannot. Satisfy. Man!"

Forster puffed on the cigar, almost frenzied, head tossed back and whirling in the darkness.

"What do *you* believe?" he demanded.

"Huh?"

"What does my gracious friend of Squeals-&-Anderson fame believe?"

The question was an incitement that burned between them like a lit fuse.

"I believe in reason," Stamer said. "I believe in capitalism."

Forster now exploded with laughter.

"Jesus Christ, how long have you been reading Ayn Rand?"

The sudden bluntness deflated Stamer's forced confidence.

"You're not a fan?" he sidled.

Forster smothered the cigar under his foot. He took a deep, somber breath then broke with a few more staccato laughs.

"The problem with dear Ayn was she was weak by refusing weakness. She could never cede control. What she feared most was unpredictability. But the market, you see, is manic-depressive, not rational. What the purists fail to realize is the whole system would come crashing down should man ever learn to stand on his own."

Stamer stayed quiet as Forster elaborated.

"Our system thrives on want. It thrives on the insecurities that riddle us. The idea of the rational, noble capitalist is flawed. *Atlas Shrugged*, for example. If Atlas shrugged, no one would care. No one cares about genius, least of all consumers. Whoever creates it, we eat it up the same. Unlike dear Ayn, I have no problem admitting weakness. I profit from it. You profit from it. I want capital to flow through the realm of feelings. Money would be nothing without emotion. It wouldn't exist in a rational world. Capitalism is a beautiful, glamorous bitch. She offers nothing but opportunity and abuse, but you don't want to be with anyone else... So tell me, using your emotions and not your reading lessons, what do you really believe in?"

Stamer's glass was empty. He reflected on the emptiness.

"I love the mountains," he said. "I guess I believe in the natural world."

Forster turned his friend around to face the party inside. The dark-haired girl in the jean jacket still stood near the window.

"Her name's Aleysha," Forster said. "She's the great great granddaughter of a Mormon prophet. Tonight will be the greatest night of her life if you can make her believe that it is."

• • •

THE TRAIL DESCENDS INTO a shaded canyon. Water flits down the hillside in a shallow rill, dives beneath the trail through a culvert, and disappears in the river below. Dorle steps toward the hillside and touches the dark green combs of a fragrant conifer, its wood a grayish hue of white.

"This is a white fir. I'm almost positive," she says. "My dad used to cut 'em for Christmas trees when I was a kid."

She steps back, hands on her hips, and ponders the specimen. Li draws near and fondles the branches as well. The two work as partners in discovery.

Stamer's thinking of that first night he met Forster. The balcony in sharp relief. Cigar smoke, splashes of wine, laughter. A woman named Aleysha. Her charcoal-tinged skin, Ute skin, arched and tapered between the black wings of an unzipped dress. And then, with a head-ache in the mousy morning light, the pleasing glide of a drab-olive sock up his bare ankle, one after the other, and the wrinkled, woolen pant leg lowered over the pale, hairy skin of his triumphant calf, one after the other.

Dorle steps back into the middle of the trail, hips hinting at motion, wanting to swivel forward, but Li's entranced by the tree, the white fir. In the squeeze of some weird silent jealousy, Stamer spots Dorle's white underwear, sweat-stained, edging just above her khaki shorts, where her blue shirt sticks to the small of her back. He's irri-tated by the sight of her splotchy skin, as if it were a contaminant to his preconceived image of female beauty. He doubts the love he felt. His doubt is a flicker then a snuffing anger toward Dorle and Li, toward himself. Feelings get up and walk away, he thinks. He walks on.

● ● ●

STAMER WAS BARELY THIRTY when he realized he'd become a snob. At the time of this realization, he was vice president of commercial services at Squeals & Anderson and had a large office on the ninth floor of the thirteen-story building.

His twenties had been consumed by this ascendancy. He'd started in residential loans and developed an impenetrable debt portfolio with the lowest rate of default in the intermountain west. When he was twenty-five, the bank made him community marketing director of

residential mortgage services and sent him up to a small corner office
on the third floor beside a defunct water cooler. His duties involved
managing advertising accounts with local media but also serving as
the department's liaison at various social functions in the city. It was
an easy job, a relaxed job, full of conferences, banquets, and schmooz-
ing, but an unfulfilling job in Stamer's mind. Recognizing the position
as the first rank in the legion of officers, he abided faithfully, and from
that point his rise to the ninth floor was more or less assured.

The day before Stamer's thirtieth birthday, the bank president
called him into his office on the topmost floor. It was an expansive
executive office that doubled as living quarters. The marble floor and
walnut molding in the lobby set the interior tones of the greater suite.
A single receptionist behind a freestanding walnut desk greeted Stamer
as he exited the elevator. Her figure was as precise as a mannequin, erect
and forward-looking in her chair, with live, lustering blond hair spilling from the seamless mold of her face.

"Mr. Stone," she said, without moving an inch or blinking an eye.
"Mr. Anderson is ready to see you now."

She pressed a button near her seat, and the dark double doors
behind her slowly opened. Stamer was surprised that she knew his
name. Her fixed head tracked him like a security camera rotating under
remote control. He imagined the same head with the smile pried open,
the mouth pumping his sex in some discreet corner of the building.

"Thank you," he mumbled as he moved forward, the wall swiping
her image from view.

The marbled hallway led to a luxurious chamber of high bay
windows overlooking Main Street. Beneath the windows stretched an
L-shaped desk with a black modern finish, behind it an empty leather
chair. On the other side of the suite, shocking the space with radical
color, were a neon-green sofa and matching love seat. A slender coffee
table gleamed with the same black finish of the desk. Stamer noticed
there were no bookcases, no books, no reading material of any kind.
The only artwork was a mass-produced print hanging above the sofa,

the same portrait of Jesus Christ that had become ubiquitous in Utah. A handsome Jesus Christ with flowing brown hair and gentle hazel eyes. A loosened robe the color of cinnamon.

A toilet flushed behind him. He turned to find a door at the end of the hallway. He heard a faucet turn on and off quickly, the whispering of hands on a towel. Then the door opened. Parley Anderson stepped into the hallway, still wiping his hands with a neon-green towel. He appeared to be lost in the task, staring at the pocked, off-white wall just above the smooth walnut wainscoting, while his hands sliced over each other in the weird green cotton. He stopped wiping, stiffened, rheumatically, then turned to Stamer with a shudder.

"Mr. Stone, I didn't know you were here. Forgive my absence. I had business to attend to."

He slipped back into the bathroom and quickly returned without the hand towel. He was a man of average height, hard-brushed reddish hair, hard-scrubbed pink skin. His face had a ticking, embittered expression, his body a halting manner. He was dressed in a fine cashmere suit of gun-metal gray, but his natural features rebelled and chafed against the finery. He seemed riddled with irritation.

"Follow me," he instructed. "I have a treat for you."

He made his way behind his desk and opened a mini fridge wedged between two filing cabinets. His hand came down on his desk with a bang, leaving a bedewed yellow bottle.

"Yoo-hoo," he announced. "It tastes like chocolate milk, but the thing is, Mr. Stone, there's not an ounce of milk in it."

Stamer wanted to laugh but was also frightened. He pondered whether the chocolate drink were part of some arcane test of the discerning class, the eccentric and well-paid. He feared someone uninitiated like himself, without college ties, might fail such a test.

"I don't think you understand," the bank president continued. "It has absolutely no milk, but it tastes like chocolate milk. You need to try some."

He unscrewed the lid and held it up so Stamer could see the brown foam on the underside.

"Please, try it."

Recalling tales of upper-management hazing, Stamer held his breath and took a drink. Exhaling, he tasted nothing but a chalky chocolate residue.

"It's good, isn't it?" insisted Mr. Anderson. "It always surprises me."

He retrieved the bottle from his inferior, tipped it up and gulped himself. When the bottle came down, he had a brown non-milk mustache.

"Delicious," he said. "Now that we're refreshed, Mr. Stone, let us discuss business. You know, as everyone in this building knows, that we've been very impressed with your performance. We'd like to make you a vice president, contingent, of course, on your willingness to join us at the top of the heap, by which I mean the ninth and tenth floors. Usually, we would have promoted you sooner, but considering you don't have a college degree, I believe the wait was appropriate."

Mr. Anderson nursed the Yoo-hoo, as if prolonging his pleasure in it, portraying himself as a connoisseur.

"That said, we believe you would make an exceptional vice president. We believe you know what it takes. Do you know what it takes, Mr. Stone?"

"I believe so," Stamer answered.

"You understand that this office is the headquarters of our entire bank, don't you?"

"Yes, sir. I know Squeals & Anderson operates nearly fifty branches in four states—Utah, California, Nevada, and New York—and holds approximately 25 billion dollars in client assets. I also know Squeals & Anderson is a publicly traded company with average earnings per share in the last twelve months of about $1.75 and offering a dividend with a robust 4 percent yield. I also know you are not only president of the company, but chairman of the board and CEO, and that you received bonus stock options last year valued at $1.3 million, if the current share price holds."

Mr. Anderson took one last sip of the Yoo-hoo, cautiously.

"Very well. It sounds like you know what you're talking about, and that's very important. I'll let you in on a little secret, Mr. Stone. Ninety-nine percent of this job is sounding like you know what you're talking about. Imagine that this whole enterprise is a hot-air balloon. My job, and the job of the executives around me, is to blow hot air into the balloon, so it keeps rising. The minute one of us fails to do so, even if letting the balloon dip just a hair, the passengers in the basket, our clients, start jumping out. Do you understand?"

Stamer imagined an immense bank of helium balloons lifting the thirteen-story building skyward. Clouds drifting past the executive windows. Parachutes hanging by the door.

"Yes, sir."

Mr. Anderson leaned back in his chair and sighed.

"Sometimes, Mr. Stone, I'm not sure how I got here. My grandfather started this bank after World War I, when no one had the courage to rub two stones together. He was a great man from a tradition of great men. He saw the value of working hard and saving money. He survived the Depression, the Second World War, and he built this bank into the powerhouse it is today.

"My own father ran this institution for three decades. He was not a great man. He was a terrible man, violent, petty, one of the worst men I've known. You wouldn't believe some of the things he pulled on the board. But rest assured, Mr. Stone, it was his board. No matter how despicable a man, this was his legacy. This bank was his family. And it's my family as well. In matters of intellect and skill, I probably have no right to be here. You could probably choose someone at random in this building with more natural aptitude for my job and position. But it still wouldn't be his position to have, would it? It's my position to have. This is my bank, my legacy, and I will protect it from riffraff if necessary. I understand you have very good instincts. You might even have the Midas touch. But do not, for one instant, think you're entitled to more than you are."

Mr. Anderson raised the empty Yoo-hoo bottle and turned it in his fingers like it were an ornament.

"I like the way you present yourself, Mr. Stone. I think you will make a fine officer of the name, but remember it is not your name. Your friend, Mr. Cutting, Mr. Forster Cutting, I don't care for. He's the riffraff I warn you about. The schemer who thinks the great families of America owe him something. I've seen it in his eyes, his rashness. He fancies himself an investor-poet. He believes he can light a fire and burn down the old rules. Can simply climb on top of that hot-air balloon we discussed, *our* hot-air balloon, and reach the stratosphere before the rest of us. Your friend is a dangerous man. Mark my words, he'll end up jumping from the top of a very tall building. I don't want him anywhere near my bank. Do you understand?"

The fierce, red earnestness of the man's face subsided into pink blotchiness. Stamer stared at the yellow bottle on the desk, nodding blankly. Mr. Anderson caught his gaze.

"I'm terribly sorry, but I'm afraid we're out of Yoo-hoo."

The following weekend, Stamer celebrated his birthday with Forster in a new Asian fusion restaurant downtown. Chefs in Oriental headbands griddled and raked meat across a heated slab of steel inset in the center of their table. Such convenience and show would characterize the 1990s, the racing decade they were now entering.

Forster's consulting contract with Squeals & Anderson had been terminated for reasons never shared with Stamer. Forster was evasive on the subject. When pressed, he chalked it up to personality differences.

"Everyone's so into computer stocks," he complained over saké. "But there's just no romance in it for me. Everyone wants to imagine this huge upside, like computers and nothing else will drive progress. But computers aren't sexy. Tell me, can you really see a man or woman falling in love with a data processor? No. Of course not. They're functional, not furniture. You don't lay your body in 'em. They're the packaging of data, not its interpretation, not its transformation. I don't care what they say. I need big, permanent things. Drills in the earth. Glass and steel in the sky. I need P/E ratios that sing. Not some dirty little machine."

Stamer slurped stir-fry with his chopsticks, remembering Squeals & Anderson was not the only client Forster had lost. Falling out of favor in certain circles, Stamer knew, could turn a whole city against a man.

His friend's weasel-like face, betraying no shame, dove into the meat and rice, devouring the greasy scraps with wild relish.

"Vegas," Forster belched. "In the new millennium, I want to be in Las Vegas. Everyone calls it 'Sin City,' but there's no greater sin than dullness."

Stamer slept fitfully later that night. He dreamed he was wandering inside a vast supermarket. It was the size of a warehouse, but it had been insulated, drywalled, with wafer-thin ceiling tiles dropped between tracts of fluorescent lighting. The walls had been textured and painted a gaudy yellow. A chintzy-white linoleum floor led him into a maze of commercial shelving. The front of each row displayed samples of inventory and oversized placards advertising discounted prices. Between the mastheads flashed aisles that were like pathways into the future, eternally lit shelves stocked with every paltry bit of matter, every shape and color succeeding one another in endless self-propagation. Then there was an opening in the rows. A plastic bin the size of a bathtub. It was wrapped in blue bunting and yellow smiley-face stickers. As though cartwheeling, Stamer tipped over the edge and fell into a pool of shrink-wrapped cartons. He sunk into the merchandise as if he were drowning. His right hand gripped the edge of the bin, while his left hand treaded the light, flimsy boxes. What the items were he couldn't tell. Each box had an incomprehensible product description on the back. On the front were blank squares, empty templates, as the cartons themselves were empty, weightless. He realized he was drowning in a bottomless pit of packaging. He screamed, but there was no sound, just expired breath. Then a squeal from beneath the shuffling cartons. He dug down by his feet and felt something hard and narrow. It slipped like a fish between the shrink-wrapped surfaces. Struggling to keep hold, he wrested it to the surface. He kicked his way out and grabbed the edge of the bin. In the superstore light, the thing was as small as a baseball card, sleek and black. It looked like plastic but felt like glass. When he turned it over in his hand, he found the source of the sound. Embedded in the surface was a screen screeching with static. The scrambled image swept across the device, over and over, until it resembled an opaque waterfall, the clouded lens of a blind man's eye.

Stamer woke up shrieking, drenched in sweat, knowing the device in his dream was the future.

He forgot about it the following week at work, when his promotion was officially announced in a nationally distributed press release. But the image started sneaking back in—the embodiment of some blind, screaming imperative—especially when he realized how bad Forster had screwed up. Rumors of his mismanagement were permeating the financial sector of the city. He'd missed big opportunities, passed on breakout tech stocks. He'd become petulant and defiant to the point of insubordination. As Stamer was rising in the moneyed ranks, Forster was falling and falling fast. In a matter of weeks, his client list became a crapshoot of wannabe venture capitalists. Somehow, he managed enough cash flow to keep intact what every socialite in the city recognized as a glamorous lifestyle. He still threw parties, traveled abroad, recited poetry while dining with friends, but his credibility was shot, at least in Salt Lake City. There was no more respect flowing from the top. He became a backroom joke.

And it was this meteoric failure that illuminated Stamer's own snobbery. It hit him later that year while he was reading a special ad supplement to the Wall Street Journal devoted entirely to wristwatches, a thin and glossy catalogue with emerging brand names like Lesson

8, Swatchican, and Taylor Coast. Exquisite dials plated with gold and platinum. Bands of brushed steel. Minute gears interlocked, needles ticking. The men in the catalogue were swathed in handsome sweaters and khaki trousers, flexing their wrists for all to see. They stared from the pages with ice-blue eyes, manufactured eyes, everything timed by the perfect click of a dial. Then he felt it, the mechanism breaking, cogless, hanging open like a wound. Suddenly the perfect posture of every magazine ad he'd ever seen shattered against his new knowledge of failure. Suddenly his association with a ruined man disgusted him. And this disgust turned to shame. And this shame to indignity.

Bewildered, enraged, he fled his apartment. It was springtime, and the night air was still cool despite a blanket of sulfurous smog hanging over the city. His mind snapped and pawed at the penny-sparkled sidewalk. He passed the bank that slept like a dull stone head amid sharper, brighter faces of other buildings. Weak light emanated from Mr. Anderson's office on the top floor. The stupid coward, he thought. He wanted to throw a rock through the windows along the street. He wanted to tear down the pillars supporting the entrance. He would rip up the foundation itself with his own hands if it meant vindicating his friend. Just imagining the destruction filled him with strange righteousness, opened a new avenue in the dark. He hurried past the bank facade, through a short alleyway, then down State Street toward the jeering neon lights of dive bars and pawnshops.

As he walked south, still angry, he felt the craving for sex swelling in his groin, the notion of release throbbing in his head. He knew of a brothel about half a mile down the street, a mid-brow sex market facilitated in the furnished basement of an Irish-themed pub. He picked up his pace. He crossed intersections against blinking red lights, hearing the ghostly vrooms of cars around him but ignorant of their danger, his blood pumping against an invisible oppressor.

Near the intersection of State Street and 900 South, a homeless Native American man approached him. He was short and husky, wearing a hunter's red flannel shirt and black sweatpants shot through with

holes. His sneakers, Velcro-strapped, were glaring white, and his hair a
tangled silvery black. In the streetlight, his coal-dark eyes glittered in a
thousand broken directions. He smelled like mud and wild mint.

"You go the bad way," the man said, his arm pointing down State
Street.

For the second time that night, Stamer was overcome by disgust.
His instincts screeched like the encased image he'd seen in his dream.
His thoughts spiked in random differentials, reflexively increasing his
own worth against the penurious object before him. He would have
kept walking if not for something in the man's eyes.

"Wizos," the man said, now pointing to Stamer's wristwatch.

Stamer held up his arm. He touched the watch's stainless steel
band, its smooth digital face. The man's eyes followed his every
movement.

"I'm sorry, what'd you call this?"

The man stepped out of the light.

"Wizos. Bad spirits. Whoosh," he dramatized with a rushing hand.
"Everywhere. In the cars. The watch. Wizos are not good for you."

The man walked to the edge of traffic, revealing several cigarette
burns on the backside of his flannel shirt. For a second, he gestured as
if to leap in front of a car. Stamer flinched. The man raised his arms in
the air as though he were summoning the atmosphere to his concern.

"Man makes these cities but can't control them. Wizos know and
won't let man go back to the good way. They feed on the man's fears."

"They're in my watch?"

The man smiled, showing black gaps in his teeth.

"My name is Red Cloud. I am Ute."

Stamer inched back on the sidewalk. The man followed him.

"Are you drunk?" Stamer asked.

"No."

He coughed and wiped his mouth with the sleeve of his shirt.
Then he started off eastward, slanted up the sidewalk.

"Come with me," he shouted back. "We should not be alone in the night."

The invitation undid something in Stamer. Standing there at the deserted intersection, he realized he'd forgotten the people in his life. His mother and father. His brother. His first love. He'd even turned against his only friend. And for what? A cold, unpeopled perch on top of a cold, unfriendly bank? He had no closeness with anyone. There was only distance, and silent devastation.

"Come with me," Red Cloud called out. "I will show you the good way."

● ● ●

FROM THE GLARING, DUSTY track a cool passage of shadow curves down beneath the trees. There's a wooden bridge, the river, the falls in the distance. The upwelling mist meets his hot flesh like a salve, dissolving his stridency, softening the aridity of his pride. He wants to touch her. He doesn't want to lose what he felt in the morning. He wants attraction to be stronger than disgust. Wholeness out of pieces.

He puts his hand on her side, feeling sweat through her shirt.

"Careful," he whispers.

She slows down and turns her head slightly. Her chin touches her bare collar bone. Her eyes cast down.

Now he's pivoting around her, his fingers sliding down her arm and off her flesh with a pluck. He moves in front of her but leaves his arm waving behind, his hand free and open for the taking. *Please, please, please.* He feels her take it, the jerk of contact, like a fish on a line, and then, adjusting to one another's touch, to one another's rhythm, they walk down to the bridge together.

● ● ●

ON A SMOGGY SPRING night in the last decade of the second millennium, Stamer Stone followed his new friend Red Cloud up the city lanes that lifted with the eastward benches of the mountains. There was a park fast asleep, shadowy turf cradled by cottonwood trees beginning to leaf. There was a neighborhood of half-lit bungalows separated by chain-link fencing, the small houses all encamped together like the pioneer model homes of Western suburbia. They passed an old high school that had high brick walls and square, sad windows without the faintest light. Red Cloud pointed to a low window which the rocks of children had busted into fang-like shards. He grumbled something about the window, but Stamer couldn't make it out. There was no explanation for the violence.

Soon they reached the boulevard that ran parallel to the foothills. Cars screamed by with low, hissing tires. Larger freight trucks reared and racketed their way to the interstate.

"You better run," Red Cloud said as he plunged into traffic, a lumbering bandit.

Before he could stop himself Stamer was chasing the man through strafing headlights. The foghorn blast of an oncoming semi made him stop and turn toward traffic. There was scalding light everywhere, omniscient in its penetration, and he thought he'd been hit when Red Cloud pulled him out of the way, the two men stumbling onto the far sidewalk.

"You crazy fool!" Stamer yelled.

"Shhh," Red Cloud warned, pointing to the tall hedges along the sidewalk. "This is the way."

The Ute parted two junipers as though the shaggy, sticky foliage were door-flaps of a tepee. The moment Stamer stepped down onto the muck of a crude trail, the city disappeared, became a distant drone. The night before them was still and silent. They traversed the periphery of an office complex, across lawn short and prim as a golf course. At the border of the grass, they entered a woody thicket around a turgid creek. The stream banks were muddy, and Stamer kept slipping as he followed Red Cloud up the drainage. The corduroy sport coat he'd grabbed on the way out of his apartment now rubbed and ripped against willow branches, his tan leather loafers caked in mire. By the time they crossed a log footbridge to the north side of the creek, Stamer's feet were numb from having sloshed around in so many tiny pools.

In a small clearing before them, a group of homeless men huddled around a campfire. In the wavering firelight, Stamer could see caverns carved out in the twisted stalks of giant willow, spaces large enough for tables and chairs and, in one hollow, an old hutch loaded with tin dishes. On the far side of the clearing an oil lantern hung from a claw of scrub oak, illuminating niches in the brush where bedrolls had been laid in relative cover. Above the encampment rose the glass Rubik's Cube of a medical research facility. Its dark cell windows glistened in the indigo sky, like the touchscreen building blocks of a futurist dream. Farther north, Stamer knew, similar structures made a glittering city of the university. But in the brush, around the creek, the city was made of pungent roots. The willow brakes were office buildings, the scrub oak multiroomed mansions, the campfire the city center. Red Cloud said something in passing to the group of men, who returned only a few hoarse words of admonishment. The flames danced away as the Ute led Stamer through a soggy maze of sedge and willow. At the end of the maze stood a single pine tree, around which Red Cloud had used a canvas tarpaulin to fashion a lean-to.

"You sit. I'll make a fire," he said.

Stamer was relieved to find an old electric blanket beneath the tarp. Sitting, he fingered the dirty-white wool, frayed into tiny clumps, and found the stiff unused cord embedded in the fabric. He watched Red Cloud pick twigs and pine needles from the base of the tree and mold them together in a small pyre. With the strike of a match and some fidgeting and blowing the pyre was soon blazing in the night. Stamer leaned back on the blanket. He let the flickering warmth of the flames liquefy his mind.

"You live here," he stated without question. "This is all you have?"

Red Cloud nodded and sat down beside the fire.

"This is all I need," he said.

He dug his hand into the pocket of his sweatpants and produced a long, narrow object wrapped in a blue handkerchief.

"I do have a knife."

He handed it to Stamer, who could instantly feel the resident grime in the cloth. Unfolding the sides he found a long, curved hunting knife. The blade was blemished but sticky-sharp when he flicked it with the tip of his finger. The handle was made of two bone plates screwed together.

"What do you have this for?"

Red Cloud patted his stomach.

"Cutting food. But I don't eat anymore. I want you to keep the knife."

"Why?"

"I'll be dead soon."

Stamer instinctively rose to challenge the statement, but then relaxed. He knew the man had no reason to lie. He turned the knife over in his hands, finding every nick in the blade, the crust of rust at the hilt.

"A man needs a good knife," Red Cloud said.

"I'm sorry for—"

"Don't. I'm in a good place."

Red Cloud drew a triangle in the air, from the willow path, to some scrawny maples near the creek, back to the solitary evergreen under which they sat.

"This is my home. I know everything about it. The plants that cover me. The birds that come in the summer and make songs for me. The grass that turns brown and dies for me. I lift up the rocks and see bugs digging holes in the ground, trying to survive. I don't feel sad for them. They're my brothers and sisters. We go on together. Like the water coming down the mountain."

• • •

HE'S BEHIND HER, AND she can feel his gaze. It has the silent, invasive force of a judgement. The way it pares her down to pieces. The way it makes her slip and question herself. It's the gaze of every man she's ever known. The gaze every woman understands is her own delineation in a story not her own. She suddenly feels his fingers on her arm, the thrill of another body, its heat and sweat and smell. Then his hand extended in space. She takes it and feels a jolt in her shoulder twinging her ribs, a knock on her bones. She can't help but smile as their hands manage a tentative, slippery grip.

They approach the bridge together. A timber-railed platform splayed among gray-white boulders and straight-boled pine trees and frantic sprays of water. The mist is like vapor off a tongue. She can see people taking pictures on the far railing against the booming backdrop of Vernal Falls. The sight makes her think of her daughter and her husband and why the ache of failed love is not as strong as it was. Maybe this man snagged in her hand, this ratchet of flesh a check on some uncertain flinging ecstasy. She wonders if they could take off together. Just like birds. Like seeds of a flower.

• • •

DORLE PLUCKED *MRS. DALLOWAY* from her father's bookshelf when she was seventeen. By that time, her parents had divorced, her mother lived in San Francisco, and her father split his time between the bars of downtown Farewell and the cellar at home—either drinking others' wine by the bottle or raking his arthritic fingers over the dry profundity of his own vintages.

Years later, Dorle would find her father's lifeless body in the same cellar, slumped over the oak workbench he'd built into the network of shelves and stone niches. It was there in the root-bitter, dust-filled dark that he'd studied himself, had found whatever satisfactions there were to find or whatever deficiencies there were to cover. His body was brittle when she found him, his skin dry and sour, and she couldn't believe that such a frail shell had housed a hot, wet, beating heart for so many years—a heart that wore down to a nub and gave one last jerk in the dark.

"Your mother," the shell told her when she was seventeen, "is better than us. She has all the things we don't have. Do you understand, honey? There are two types of people in the world, poor people and rich people. Most people in between lie to themselves about it. They want to be rich so bad they're willing to give up their own happiness. Everything they do is about finding a way in. But we do okay by ourselves, don't we, honey? We can be happy with what we have."

Dorle didn't understand much of *Mrs. Dalloway*. The characters came and went. The descriptions swelled beyond the curve of her interest. But there were parts that entertained her. That first flush of attraction. That first kiss on the terrace that burned through the understory of the house and set the fence on fire. There were revelations that touched something on the other side of herself. They fanned open like sunlight and filled her with warm, vague meaning. Something about a cornucopia. A roundness, a fullness, an exquisite plenitude. She remembers thinking about the restaurant where she worked in that way: the overwhelming fulfillment of serving food, the customers talking and laughing as they waited for their meals, happy in hunger, arms sweeping across the tables, communicating the breadth of their mutual appetites. She would bring the stand in one hand, and the tray of food, still smoking from the kitchen, on the upturned palm of the other. Their eyes would meet, always adoring, grateful eyes, then yelps of excitement, a circle of involuntary smiles. In those moments of recognition, she would know her true power—the people under her brief but beneficent care would never be happier.

The restaurant was called Michael's. It was an above-average diner housed in the wraparound corner of a two-story, redbrick building in downtown Farewell, a block east from the bridge that spanned the creek and the sulfurous, gold-sedged pools of the hot springs.

Michael Irons Jr. was a second-generation proprietor. He'd inherited the restaurant from his father in 1968, the same year as the Tet Offensive in South Vietnam, and the same year Michael Irons Sr., a Midway veteran who'd opened the eatery two decades earlier, decided to end his life with a Colt .45 pistol. The poorly written suicide note blamed the madness of all-consuming war, but Michael Jr. knew there was more to it.

The town had already started to change by then. More of the city was creeping in. After the first Michael passed, two marginal vineyards were purchased within a year of each other and supposedly revitalized. Tasting rooms replaced the hardware store and butcher shop. The lumber building became an art gallery. Historic homes downtown, ingenuous, even crummy, were suddenly valuable. Although new money swept in like a rising tide, it did not lift all boats. Those who sold out did not stay. Those who stayed bought in, believing in their own inexhaustible wealth. Others like Michael Irons Jr. remained skeptical, struggling to adapt rather than flee. He participated in the new market but did so grudgingly. He printed new menus with fancier fonts and higher prices. He installed wainscoting on the open walls between the booths. But everything else—the splintered floorboards, the chipped countertops, the actual ingredients scrambled and smoking on the griddle—remained the same. He would not change these things, and over time this visible, tactile, olfactory resistance to change became the diner's signature charm.

Dorle had gone to school with Michael Jr.'s son before dropping out her senior year. Like his father, Jason Irons stood tall and skinny and stoic. His gangling limbs could be graceful in deliberate motion. His curly red hair, like shag carpet, could appear to cushion the wooden nod of his wooden face. The skin of the face was freckled and forever sunburnt, the nose forever peeling, crusted pink, with undertones of burnt sienna. Like his father, he possessed a mild sense of humor—

both willing to tell and take jokes—but also a harsher repudiation of
the world, a sudden stern manner that caused the gangling limbs to
stiffen in uprightness.

He had known Dorle in school as shy boys know pretty girls in
small towns. They might have hung out once or twice through mutual
friends, but never intimately. He was a quasi-loner who dipped into the
small circles of working-class kids which comprised the nascent service
class of Farewell. She was a social chameleon engaged in parties, saturated by the material culture of a particular clique for a short period of
time. The straining hues of the art club. The banal cigarette smoke of
the dropouts. The slick muscle cars of the athletes. It was the second
group that eventually claimed her. Though bright, she had never been
a good student. As her mother's disappearance became permanent and
her father's depression deepened, Dorle realized there was nothing else
to do but work. She came to appreciate money, not because she was
exceedingly greedy, but because she realized the things she loved in
the world—pearl earrings, chocolates, Christmas trees—were not free.
These things that filled her up all came at a cost.

She knew her father would never sell their home, and she doubted
he had title to it anyhow. Occasionally she let herself imagine that her
mother would appear at the threshold with gifts and promises. But the
dreams always failed. She would walk down the hill behind the house,
through thistle gone to seed, spurge like a hoary clamp, and into the
thicket around the creek where she'd once seen a red deer lift its antlers
in the smoky light or at least had believed a story about such a thing.
She would walk along the creek, sensing fate in the sod-built banks,
the fallen trees, the things that could no longer move. She would dip
her toes in the clear pebbled pools and watch the water for some ripple
of release. Water was her anodyne. It always had been. As a child, after
bingeing on Christmas cookies, lying for hours in her parents' claw-
foot tub. As a teenager, after losing her virginity, standing alone in the
hot, ferric streams of the shower. That time, water soothed the feel-

ing inside that was worse than sin, the way he'd cut through her and discarded her.

Jason was different, though. She'd worked at the diner for weeks before really noticing the lonely, meager smile in the service window. She noticed his arm swinging out and down with the delivery of each order, his hand committing each dish so tenderly to the scraped-up, egg-white countertop, as if laying children to sleep. The dishes became families in her serving tray, which she wheeled through the diner with novice grace, her ashen blond hair yanked down in a haphazard ponytail, loose strands of it sticking to the neck-strap of her black apron. The food would come off her tray steaming and quickly disappear in the mouths of her growing fan base. They would forgive any misstep, any spill, the adorable disorder of her hair, her thin, trembling features, as long as she fulfilled what had been promised.

It was a pageant she and Jason performed every night. They took breaks as time allowed, but rarely together. She ate very little, a couple of fries from the basket, some dry cereal from the pantry. Noticing this, Jason made her dinner one night.

"There was no burger in this order," she said.

The familiar arm, coppery with freckles, was fixed rodlike in the service window, the unfamiliar smile a cleft tenderness in the sunburnt patina of his face.

"I made it for you," he said, and his voice was plain and straight and solid. She didn't know if she'd ever heard him speak. It was an edifying voice, each syllable like the quiet knock of a carpenter at work in a church.

"Half a pound of beef," he said.

He turned and vanished behind the wall before she could thank him. She wanted to tell him she couldn't eat it now because a table was waiting for their order. She pushed herself up on her tiptoes and poked her head through the window. She was going to tell him to wrap the unexpected gift in tinfoil, but there was no one in the kitchen. When she returned to her feet, the kitchen doors were swinging open and Jason was heading into the dining room with her orders on a tray.

"I got it," he called back. "You go eat before it gets cold."

The moment was unexpected, a broken inertia. She sat alone at the counter, contemplating the humongous hamburger in her hands. A cocktail of condiments dripped on her knuckles. Then she lifted the meat to her lips. Sesame seeds in the bun crackled as her teeth came down in the first bite; grease and blood squirted the inside of her cheek. She chewed. She swallowed. The masticated glob of food slid down her throat and landed in her stomach with a warm thud, an intimation of plentitude. She'd been so hungry, so empty. The first bite was a kiss of blood, and now she turned on the hamburger like a starved vampire. Its juices lacquered her mouth as she worked the food inside her. She could taste the pungent, cloven flesh of an onion, piquant, burning, then the cool tang of a pickle. Swallowing the last bite, she yanked paper napkins from a nearby dispenser, wiping her hands and chin. She wanted to thank Jason. She wanted to cry. She'd never been so full.

• • •

LOVE BEGINS WITH INFATUATION, she knows, and leads to a lifetime of discomfiture. She watches the man who has let his hand fall away from hers. He is walking toward the restrooms on the other side of the bridge. He is putting a river between them, a raging whiteness. The scent of him has deserted her. She throws her eyes to the forest. A dream of trees in the skull of the canyon. The pines, the firs, the oaks, the flowering dogwoods and white alders. Smells and textures like the intricate foliage of memory. What was it he said to her before leaving? He said he'd be right back. Or was it something more forceful, more committed? *I won't leave you.* The trees dripping mist she can't tell from tears. She's not crying but wants to cry. Everything torn green and gray, people swarming the bridge like ants.

"I wish I could paint you," Li says, stepping into view. "The way you look right now."

His hands form a square to frame her.

"Your hair is like the stringy forest. Your eyes are full of light, standing there waiting for him."

Dorle blushes, cheeks tingling.

"That's a weird thing to say."

She's staring at his face. It's burnished so smoothly it doesn't look real. Like a bronze head behind a sheet of glass in a museum.

"Why would you want to paint me?"

All at once she sees an edge in his presentation she hasn't seen before. His eyes are onyx, but there's movement within. Mute flashes of lightning. Redness.

"Because of your beauty. I'd like to catch it before it's too late."

"Too late?"

Dorle wonders if he's making a pass at her. She realizes the two of them haven't been alone since the hike began.

"Before the moment's gone," he clarifies.

Her anxiety shifts to the shoulders of the ants.

"I didn't know you were an artist."

"I used to be an artist," he sighs. "I wish I could be an artist again."

Dorle further considers his appearance. Of the three of them, he's the best-dressed. "When were you an artist?"

"In China. I was an artist in Beijing."

"How long ago?"

"It's been, hmm, two years since I left."

"Okay. You already forgot how to be an artist?"

Her question seems to slap him. She doesn't know why his face is stiffening.

"I'm sorry. I didn't mean anything by it."

He shakes his head.

"It's nothing. I came here to paint again, to find a new way. I just haven't found it yet."

"I'm sorry. This day has been weird for me."

Dorle anticipates the return of his canny smile, but it doesn't return. There's something else, she thinks. Something deeper. He's been hurt, or has hurt someone. She suddenly senses the depth of his sorrow. It's like the bottom of the river. The rushing underside of the static world everyone around her takes for granted. She feels herself slipping.

● ● ●

SHE NEVER READ ANOTHER book after *Mrs. Dalloway*. Herr Wasser's book collection disappeared with the house after his death. The house was sold in probate, and everything inside, if not sold, was boxed and relegated to an industrial storage unit on the outskirts of new suburbia. Frau Wasser had signed the papers and closed the deal. Proceeds flowed to creditors first and then to herself. Because the value of the property had risen dramatically, she was able to take a significant profit. Herr Wasser had done nothing to protect his assets. There was no will, no trust. The daughter, the sole heir, had learned in court that her parents never officially divorced. Her father had not been able to quit the promise of his marriage, whatever minuscule warmth that promise provided, and now there was nothing left.

Dorle married Jason in January of 1984, shortly after her father died. She was twenty years old. The hole inside her had been growing for months like a reverse cancer, hollowing and aching, the hours of her days deteriorating in cold, vague pain. Even the holidays, the season she loved most of all, couldn't deactivate the vacuum inside. It was the first Christmas her father had not taken her into the mountains to cut down a tree. She'd persisted, but he wouldn't leave the cellar. Two days after Christmas, he was dead.

The night of his final refusal—in fact the last time she spoke to him—Dorle stormed down the hill behind the house. In her hand was the rusted saw she'd grabbed from his pegged tool rack, which, hewn from fresh pale plywood, belied the deep dark rotting timbers holding up the house. Fuck him, she thought. Fuck him. The saw's crusted teeth bit her palm as she slipped in a patch of dead grass and mud, the ground giving way like a scab. Recovering, she watched as blood twirled down her wrist. Weird that the thrill of pain had cut through pain. She licked the blood from her skin. Metallic. Not unlike the hamburger Jason had cooked for her. She turned the saw upside down and split her pinky on the serrated blade. She watched the blood trickle in limp rivulets and then sucked her finger until the bleeding stopped and a stinging, whitish slit remained.

She moved to the base of one of the Austrian pines Herr Wasser had planted between the creek and vineyard. The bark came off in chunks as she sawed. She could see the wet gleam of sapwood. Just as her wrist and forearm cramped, the tree's last ring gave, and the whole creature crashed to the ground.

She couldn't drag it herself. She hiked back up to the house and called Jason. When he arrived in his tan Toyota pickup, small and low compared to her father's truck, it was raining.

"I need help carrying a Christmas tree," she told him through his cracked window. "You can drive around back."

She pointed out the path in the rain. Her wet arm was the color of plaster, her wet hair like live wires, sparking faintly in the headlights. The dark bulges of her breasts, beneath the saturated shirt, stayed in Jason's head as he followed the dirt road around the vineyard. She walked to the house first and then met him by the felled tree, a clean towel draped over her shoulders.

Jason put the truck in neutral and kept the engine running and the headlights on. He unrolled the window.

"How does your dad feel about cuttin' this tree down?"

Her eyes caught the headlights in a bright, seething glow.

"He doesn't care what I do."

She shifted her back to the car while Jason considered what she said. Through the streaked windshield he could see her shoulders shaking.

"Hey Dorle, I'm just telling ya it would be a waste of time to drag that thing up to the house."

She turned, suddenly, dropped the towel, and rushed to the truck. Before the passenger door clanked shut behind her, or the cabin light dimmed, she had straddled him in the driver's seat and begun sucking his mouth the same way she'd sucked blood from her finger. He grabbed her hips, pushing her back first, then gradually yielded, accepting the suffocation of her tongue with a jarred mouth. She only stopped to shuck off her shirt and bra. In the dim light of the dashboard his hands found her milky breasts. Rain smacked the windshield. He thought he was going to die. He thought he was dying when she unzipped his fly and shoved him inside herself. She began climbing his body, climbing then falling, rocking and moaning, opening and closing her tiny wet door. Within seconds, uncontrollably, he jerked upward and came inside her. His breath sputtered, a signal to stop, but she didn't stop. She ground harder into his groin.

"Sta...stop," he stuttered. "You're hurting me."

When she didn't quit, he pushed her over to the passenger seat.

"What the hell?"

He shook his head and struggled to zip up his jeans.

"I told ya you were hurtin' me."

She stared at him suspiciously, then bared her small white teeth.

"Get out," she said.

"What? It's my truck."

"Get out!" she screamed.

Dumbfounded, Jason looked at the dashboard. The incandescent speedometer. The sound of his own breath. The rain splatting and plashing on the windshield. He turned off the engine and removed the keys.

"I just—"

"Get out," she said.

He left the driver's door open and stood nearby in the rain.

"Just so ya know, you're fuckin' crazy," he said.

He thought he saw her smile before she reached over and slammed the door. He stayed that way, in the rain, for almost half an hour before she let him back in. By that time, she knew she'd won, for he was utterly humiliated and utterly in love.

When her father died after Christmas, money was sent in the mail for cremation. There were no services. She scattered the ashes in the creek behind the house then fled to Lake Tahoe with Jason. They got married in a chapel in Nevada. They spent their wedding night in a casino that served free cocktails. She would remember the first hour sitting at a blackjack table pounding shots of tequila and losing a month's worth of tips. She wouldn't remember the rest of the night when her pounding got louder, each drained glass coming down on the bar like a pistol butt, ringing and shattering Jason's insulated buzz. She wouldn't remember cursing at the bartender when he cut her off, or Jason dragging her to the elevator and clenching her wrists when she screamed and tried to hit him. She would remember, much later, something she'd seen in that small space, a vague splendor, like a gossamer sheet fluttering against the ceiling, the white walls of the elevator shimmering into shadow—the very moment oblivion washed over her, the faintest pulse of ecstasy lost to darkness.

Blacking out was an experience she'd relive over and over again in the last days of their marriage. The early days were easier. They rented a newly constructed town house a few blocks from the diner. It was a slice of pastel-colored pie, a gabled wedge of custard-yellow siding with white-trimmed windows. The carpet inside was clean-smelling but cheap to the touch, thin and hard. Composite cabinetry hung in the kitchen. No crown molding. No hardware. The paper veneers, imitations of oak grain, were already peeling. In the unit's one bathroom, the faux-tile linoleum had been stretched over the subfloor like a tacky adhesive bandage. For Jason, who'd grown up in an old bungalow his father had refused to renovate, the new home was a tidy upgrade. For Dorle, who'd grown up in the decaying airs of estate and pedigree, the new home felt like a pathetic downgrade. They spent a weekend moving in their belongings, clothing, cassette tapes, one stereo between them, and dishes that didn't match each other. Dorle had kept an oak dresser from the estate sale, one of the only items her mother had bequeathed her.

The day they moved it in, she accidentally dropped her end, causing Jason to lose his grip. The dresser slammed against the floor.

"Shit," Jason hissed.

He managed to stand it upright in the middle of the bedroom, a monolith complementing the bare mattress leaning against the far wall.

"I don't know what you want," Jason said.

"I want it in the closet. I don't want my underwear out in the open."

"Really?"

"I want my clothes in the closet. I want to put other things in our room."

"Like what?"

"Stuff we buy. I'd like a vanity set."

She pictured the pearl earrings in her mother's vanity set.

Jason pointed to the closet.

"We got mirrors right there."

Embedded in the sliding closet doors were large mirror panels. The couple reflected there, looking at themselves, appeared to be mismatched. The craning redhead, built like a crooked arrow, stood disjointedly and sad. The snappy blonde, built like a sparrow, regarded herself with a jittery turn of the head, lips perking in a smile.

"It's not the same thing," she said.

Jason saw how beautiful she was. Despite all her mental hangups, she was radiant in youth. She embodied the essence of a flame he could never quite grasp. He doubted she even knew she had it. It was there, then gone. She would turn away, and the heat would vanish, not unlike the fading wet of a kiss. He didn't know how to preserve it, or even how to point it out. It was something he couldn't articulate but could feel like electricity priming the deepest membrane of his being whenever she was close.

"I want to put the dresser in the closet," she said. "It will fit. You can make it fit."

He thought about giving her more. He knew his father wanted him to buy the business when both were ready, but he knew the diner would provide only so much. The thought of selling it disturbed him. He flinched at the reddened, stick-figure image of himself in the mirror. He would try his best, he thought. He loved her, and that would be enough.

● ● ●

WHAT IS IT? WHAT *is it she wants?*

Stamer's hot amber urine splashes on the shit below. The waste has a weather of its own: shade, heat, vapor, flies. He's sweating as he wrings the last drop from himself. He closes the toilet lid and sanitizes with Purell from a wall dispenser. The alcohol fumes make his eyes smart. Sitting on top of the toilet, he takes out his notebook. *What is it she wants?* He saw it in her eyes on the bridge. Eyes open and wild and aching from within. He's felt it himself, that hunger for substance, not materialism or anything as vulgar as the two briefcases in his tent, but a much deeper desire, a yearning for the fountain itself—immanence—life fulfilled without deficit. *Less than all cannot satisfy man.*

Ensconced in the thick, miasmic air, gnats whining, he begins to write.

We are mostly objects. But there's something in us that unifies the world.

His cheap ballpoint pen blots blue then scratches the paper. He rubs the tip of it against the corner of the page until the ink returns, flowing, shining, like electrical currents.

Like the light I saw dancing on the water. Red Cloud found it. Maybe that's as close as we get. This morning a ranger told me about a man killed by lightning. It wasn't true, but it was a warning.

He sees Forster, spiky-haired, sunburnt, tearing through file cabinets in the high executive office of the Bengal Tower in Las Vegas. He's cursing and shredding documents as lightning and thunder cackle over the city, as the sky outside turns from gray to black, humming with malevolence.

• • •

THE NIGHT OF THEIR first wedding anniversary, Dorle got drunk on vodka. She'd asked for pearl earrings, but Jason had given her a pair of dangling silver hearts instead, explaining that funds were low, rent was going up, and that his father needed money to visit a cardiologist. Michael Irons Jr. had barely survived his first heart attack and was struggling to pay off the hospital bill.

"We were supposed to go to the city," Dorle said. "You promised to take me to the city on a real date. I'm sick of eating at the same place we work."

"I promised I would, and I will. But I can't right now. My dad is sick. What do you want me to do, let him die?"

Dorle detected something false in his compassion, the slightest subterfuge. Denying her wishes in practical terms provided him some tacit officiating power. She went to the kitchen and found the fifth of vodka in the drawer beneath old bills. Jason followed her. She began taking sips. He watched her with hardened eyes but kept his distance.

"I just wanted the fucking earrings," she said. "So we can't go to the city. Okay, fine. But why can't I get just one thing I ask for? I don't ask for much."

She twisted the bottle to her lips and sucked.

"I see women every day from the city driving their Mercedes right past the restaurant," she said. "They walk around with their friends and have a great time. Sometimes they're with men, and they look serious, like they're in love—"

Jason's throat constricted. He'd always feared she didn't love him as much as he loved her.

"They're always wearing nice jewelry," she continued, her voice now wavering with the rush of alcohol in her blood. "How do you think that makes me feel? I feel worthless. I feel stupid. Like I'm stuck in this place and can't get out."

Each word tightened the vise around his heart. He knew he was stuck, too, though in a different way.

"I bought what I could afford," he said.

She took one more sip and put the bottle on the counter. She let her head loll back till her eyes caught the long fluorescent bulb of the kitchen ceiling.

"Tsss," she uttered without moving her head.

"Dorle, I was taught to live within my means."

Her eyes slid from the droning ceiling light to her husband's quietly pained face.

"You make me sick," she said.

• • •

THEY CONGREGATE ON THE bridge beneath the falls, thousands of people every day. They're from different countries, different races, but all one species bound by their desire to climb and break through the mist. The river runs as a revelation through their lives. It shows the long, sinuous dispersions of the past, the surge and swirl of present anxieties, and the future cascading down upon them with more force and determination than they'd care to admit. Their choices, the choices they make in their lives, are like stepping stones across the water: bridges they build and cling to. While some will make it to the lighted peaks beyond, others will disappear in the whirlpools of time.

Where the lower section of the trail bows outward to catch a small stream—one of several drainages carved in the canyon wall—a woman in a red shirt rests in the shadow of a gnarled live oak, the tree hanging from the slope like a twisted inquiry into space and time, individuation, gravity. Her shirt bears the image of an American flag. She puffed up the image moments before when passing a group of Indian women. Their skin, she noticed, had the reddish brown hue of cinnamon. Two of the women had red dots on their forehead, and the eldest was wearing a maroon sari. Disgusting people, she thinks. The brides of convenience store clerks, she thinks. And her husband, her ex-husband—though divorced she still considers him her stock—is a civil engineer who built levees and retention ponds throughout the state of Missouri. Yes, yes, she takes great pride in his work. A patriot, she thinks. These people have no respect, she thinks. Men like my husband built this country.

Still, when passing the three women, she couldn't help but notice how thin they were, especially the youngest of the three. It infuriates her now thinking a man like her ex-husband, a stalwart of American infrastructure, might find such a woman attractive. Go back to your slums, she snaps in her head. This park's not for you.

Her thick thighs tremble with fatigue. She can see them coming around the corner of the mountain. She wants to scream. She fears she'll pass out if she keeps hiking, but she can't let them catch up. Desperate for advantage, she scrambles ahead. She wills her legs forward, numb, heavy, but she can do it. She can take small steps, baby steps, all the way to the bridge—as long as they don't catch up!

On the other side of the canyon, where granite cliffs lift from the green slope, darkly wetted by the mist, an elderly British couple climbs the moistened staircase hewn into the mountain long ago by enterprising men. Like most enterprising men, they're dead now. But they did chisel these pedestrian steps into pristine stone. They did anchor themselves from cliff-dwelling pines, rogue oaks, to swing across the faces of stone in some ludicrous and manly ballet, pulleys singing with the weight of their tools.

The British man now reaches out to brace the faltering rump of his wife.

"Oh, thank you," she says.

Her accent is a doozy. A balloon deflating. An umbrella blown inside out. A decapitated flower, a bowl of water. He feels her plumpness oozing between his fingers. He grumps forward, humps up. His knees itch and chatter.

"Oh, dear!" she shudders, and her quavering exclamation is a dew drop rippling the pools of his old desire.

It becomes hard, the head of a match striking the stone, a rip of fire as he remembers how they passed so many Americans on the trail—younger people, stronger people—how they burned inside together to get by them. Nevada Falls by lunchtime was their plan, but no, they won't make it, at least not in time to eat the summer sausage and rye crackers and smelly cheese and currant jelly and cabernet he packed for their picnic. But he'll find a spot above Vernal Falls, beneath Nevada Falls, perhaps near Emerald Pool, yes, a perfect spot between the falls, where grass grows knee-high on the banks of the deep pools in the shade of the pine trees and purple wildflowers unfurl their tiny trumpets to herald the return of something magnificent but forgotten. On the boulders around the pools the spongy moss will be as green as Ireland yet warm like the rest of California. Truly incredible, he thinks. Even in the highest glades the ground is saturated with sun. Even now in this misty canyon sunlight penetrates the air. How long has it been since they made love? How long has it been since he got a blow job? Five, ten years? He gives his missus a ruddy nudge, then steps up and takes her weight with all he's got left. If she falls, they'll fall together— down to their splendid death in the glorious sunlight of California. His mouth hunts her ear, the sticky threads of her hair. He locks onto her like a tyrant, pumping with desire, tasting her flesh, the tang of her sweat, until a crass whisper rasps from his lips: "I love you."

• • •

LOVE ITSELF, ITS FEELING, its depth, its direction, all changed for Jason Irons in the spring of 1995.

Dorle's drinking had gotten worse. Some nights, he fought her. One night, he threw a bottle of peppermint schnapps he'd found in her vanity desk against the backside of their bedroom door. The cymbal-like explosion startled him with the sharpness of its sound, a tinkling shower of glass and liquor. Dorle began crying. She went and slid down the walls in the corner of the room like a prisoner finally surrendering to the confines of her cell. Jason stood over her, silently, with the inverse power of her failure, a power that rose as she fell. It had been building inside him for years. Cornered, whimpering, Dorle could tell he'd begun to imagine his life without her.

She promised to change. She vowed to stay out of the bars downtown and to join a local support group. The promise ushered in a brief period of sobriety. They found relative peace in the flow of work and home and sleep and sex. The latter, though, was still divisive. Jason wanted a child, Dorle didn't. Every time he brought it up, she grew angry. She swore she wouldn't bring a child into such a miserable world. He knew she meant not the world at large, but their world, the world of their own creating. By their tenth anniversary, he'd had enough. He threatened to withhold sex unless she agreed to have a kid. They'd been using condoms, and when he made the threat—abruptly, ridiculously—she grabbed the box of condoms from their nightstand and threw it in the trash.

"If you won't fuck me, then I'll find someone who will," she told him.

He quickly capitulated.

"Sorry. Don't even say that."

She smirked, then took off his pants and worked him into a mount. He thought of their first night together in his truck, when the wild rain had beat against the windshield.

"You need to learn how to fuck me good, Jason," she said, riding him harder and harder. "I always need someone to fuck me good."

He came quickly, with a pinched quiver, and realized she'd never gotten the condoms out of the trash.

In the following days at the diner, Jason thought men were smiling at him through the service window. Men from town. Former classmates. Some known to frequent the same bars as Dorle whenever she relapsed. Their smiles seemed suggestive, poisonous. One man, an urban refugee who'd bought a second home in Farewell, actually winked at him. A regular at the diner, he was not an attractive man, but Jason had learned he was a wealthy man. The wink was enough to make him paranoid. The day it happened, he let the man's burger burn on the griddle. Then he spat on the buns. He slapped together the sabotaged meal and charged through the kitchen doors, determined to ask Dorle what was going on. Before he got a foot in the dining room, Dorle stopped him. He could see she'd been crying. The corners of her eyes were pink.

"I'm pregnant," she said. "I guess you got what you wanted."

Seven months later, the black-boned hills of Farewell were green in their navels. Spring's green sparks had spread through the wintered straw and slowly set the hills ablaze with new life.

Dorle screamed in her hospital gown. Her teeth gnashed the air.

Jason felt calm standing between the nurses and doctors. His head was as clear as a lake on the edge of the world. He could swim in any direction, he thought, away from the pain. He could leave her forever and still be happy. But something called him back. The shore was riven with blood. And whatever pieces of his love remained were forming a new head, ears, eyes, nose, mouth—a small and gasping cry. There was warmth in the cry. It called him back. Dangling limbs. Breath. It called him back. A new voice, vivid and desperate, stammering on life's strange shore.

Jason picked up his baby, his precious Dora. He knew there was no going back into the clear, cool water of his dreams. He would stay. For better or worse, he would stay.

• • •

STANDING ON THE BRIDGE, Dorle can't escape a dark swell of regret. She keeps her eyes on the far end of the bridge, anticipating Stamer's return. The water rushing on either side of her seems arbitrary, unable or unwilling to cleanse the dark feeling from her body. It's a dense, insurmountable feeling. Other people on the bridge rout it by their sheer presence, push on her memories until the images separate in layers.

Dora's sand-colored hair. The sun-dappled lightness of her body.

The screech and smoke of car brakes. Pavement wet with blood. A crumpled Santa hat.

The oaken desks and benches of the courthouse. The cracked, seething ember of the judge's face. The scalding heat of his voice. The yellow-haired reporter scribbling in her notebook.

Concrete floor. White brick walls. Metal toilets. Food trays smelling like rubber. Prayers tasting like rain.

You're not alone, the guard says.

His furry face, his black beard.

You're a liar, she says.

Come anytime, he says.

No, she won't go to Sunday services. She won't go anywhere. And beneath that prison floor, beneath this wooden bridge, she intuits some crude mechanism of fate—a lever of choice and consequence, stuck, immobile. Her mistakes seem so deep, so grave, that even if the river were to wash the whole world away, her mistakes would remain.

She can't see him. She fucking hates him. The river rages beneath her. She fucking hates him. The wood of the railing slivers her hand, thinly burning, almost erotic. God, she's going to hyperventilate unless she pulls herself together. She scratches both palms.

"Are you okay?"

She shakes her head. Li puts a hand on her shoulder.

"Let's go sit down."

"Where is he?"

"Stamer?"

"He said he'd come back."

Li looks to the other side of the bridge. The newly discovered distance draws a breezy sadness settling inside him like a damp feather.

"Let's find a seat," he tells Dorle.

She takes his hand. They sit on a bench near the water fountain. Hikers lift Nalgene bottles and CamelBak bladders to trembling spouts of potable water. He pats her knee.

"We should wait. I'm sure he's coming back."

He's not sure at all. He watches her watery blue eyes glisten like wet, red-veined quartz. The skin at the corners of her eyes shows slight striations, like her face is being stretched by the same forces shaping the mountains around them. Geologic time. The helplessness of stone. Suddenly he sees Danyu's face back in the city, thousands of miles away, years ago, streaks of platinum-red hair flashing in the oriental dark. Then the knife, the shriek. He shivers inside.

• • •

LI'S FATHER WAS A smoker. At the top of every hour, he would leave his study, his files and secret compartments, and walk outside to the courtyard. There was a chipped marble bench beneath an overgrown weeping willow where he would sit, light a cigarette, and smoke ponderously. The white smoke would rise and twirl around the pale tendrils of the tree, and the man sitting there would become more wraith than father, a floating presence periodically sharpening in profile, turning toward the young eyes watching from the window.

Li—Huo Li is his full name—grew up in the poor hutong that rambled mazelike between the southeast corner of Tiananmen Square and the Temple of Heaven. It was an ancient maze of narrow alleyways that connected hundreds of traditional courtyard homes. While similar neighborhoods to the north had been preserved, had been polished by the state, made clean and prosperous, the hutong to which Li belonged languished in a forgotten realm, having missed both revitalization and the wrecking ball. It was a lost dimension of crumbling grayish brick walls and flaking black roof tiles and drooping, poorly spliced power lines. From the courtyard rooftops, children could see the new skyscrapers of the capital. They could see new shopping malls rising like faux palaces, pillared and spotlighted, and new restaurants on the lakefronts west of the Forbidden City, glowing lime-green and cherry-red.

The same kids gained snatches of the new world when biking to school. Spinning through the touristy streets outside their neighborhood, they absorbed, if only partially, the racing traffic and noise, the bright colors of billboards and storefronts, the snap and jauntiness of new clothes worn by people who didn't look that different from themselves. Yet no matter how exciting the city beyond the hutong, despite all its kaleidoscopic offerings, the children returned every evening to deteriorating walls and greasy, gauntly parents, to what each would later learn in life was often called poverty: the state of being poor, unimportant, and unconnected.

The adults of the hutong did their best to ground the children. They criticized the new city, told each other Mao would have never stood for it, and told their children that the *real* Chinese were themselves. They claimed royal stock. Li's mother swore the Huo clan originated with the noble brother of an ancient emperor. But the truth was none of them felt worthy. The district of Chongwen had always been poor. Even during dynastic rule, it had housed brothels and gambling parlors prohibited in the imperial court. Li's father, for example, had lived his entire life in the hutong. Every day, as a devoted employee of the government, he pedaled his single-gear bicycle to the vast, Soviet-inspired compounds around Tiananmen Square. But he never actually stepped foot in what was left of the Forbidden City. Every obnoxious Westerner with a passport could see what he would not allow himself to see. Because he felt unworthy.

Li's father started out as a rickshaw driver. In 1968, during the Cultural Revolution, a local splinter of the Red Guards inducted him into their cadre. He'd never been particularly revolutionary, nor did he demonstrate thorough knowledge of Maoist thought, but he looked and acted like a peasant—bowed his head to others, spoke only when spoken to—and this meekness, this proletariat image, was more important than any recitation of doctrine. Plus, he knew the city. He knew the ancient hutong routes. The group tapped him as a driver first, and then, discovering the power of his trustworthy yet strangely disarming face, used him to interrogate others. He was taught how to sit across the table from an enemy and say nothing, how to make a show of Mao's Little Red Book, perhaps slide it across the table, and do nothing but wait. What followed in almost every instance astonished him. Men who looked no different from himself excoriated themselves for having capitalist thoughts. One broke into tears and confessed to a silly dream of opening a tea shop in New York City. Another jumped out an open window, falling four stories before landing on a car. That man didn't die but was paralyzed for life.

Li's father quickly realized the power he had over others, though he didn't understand the power. He didn't know what group leaders wanted with the information he procured, but he did understand that he'd become indispensable. His reputation grew in the right circles. Years later, when the revolution ended in ignominy, when most of his comrades were shipped off to the countryside for reeducation, he was offered a job in the government. The job allowed him and one former comrade to stay in Beijing.

That comrade was Li's mother. She'd been a university student, the only girl in the cadre, and she both thrilled and terrified Li's father.

Beneath her general prettiness was a specific ugliness, a viciousness that made a whip of her crow-black hair. During the revolution, she had frequently interrupted his interrogations, sometimes using the Little Red Book to slap the accused across the face. She used the same aggression on her future husband, though modulated differently, to win his affection, to stoke and claim his desire. He didn't know why she chose him in this way. He sensed she was guided by some instinct of self-preservation. But he never questioned her loyalty. When the fever of revolution broke, she remained in Beijing as his wife.

By the 1980s, Li's father had become one of the most effective domestic agents of the Ministry of State Security. His work took him undercover to almost every precinct in the city. He worked hard at infiltrating safe houses, havens of pro-democracy activism located in otherwise benign neighborhoods. He also infiltrated the universities, interviewing teachers and students, intercepting newsletters that were, most often, circulated in school libraries. He made a special task of befriending newspaper editors, gradually, stealthily questioning them, drawing out long, latent self-criticisms, and then, when so weakened, re-embracing them and transforming them into allies. Smooth, compliant messaging from the press was his goal. And his goal was always met. Although he was a stoic, self-contained man, his reputation grew into something fearsome. Those whose inner circles he penetrated never suspected him a state operative. His quiet and terse manners belied his motives and his ruthlessness. Only later, after being exposed, did they reckon his true power. Eventually he earned the nickname Luduan. Like that mythical creature, he discerned truth and falsehood with uncanny, seemingly supernatural precision. The silent certainty of his eyes forced out lies living beneath the surface of another. A simple tap of his hand on a table could summon the deepest confession. He had other tools at his disposal, but his presence alone was usually effective.

As Li grew into adolescence, he began asking his father about his work. One night after dinner he asked him what his job was.

"My job is to defeat the enemy's cunning," Luduan answered, with an uncharacteristic amount of pride in his voice. "The enemy is deceptive and supremely selfish."

"Who is the enemy?" Li asked.

The question was innocent in its curiosity. Still, it narrowed Luduan's eyes, halted the progression of pride in his voice.

"Careful, son, it is a mistake to think the enemy is a person. The enemy is not a person. It is a thing that can corrupt any person."

The Tiananmen Square protests of 1989 embarrassed the Ministry of State Security on an international stage. While Luduan's comrades scrambled to smother any vestige of sympathetic press, to hunt down and punish those who'd helped smuggle photos out of the country, he was assigned an unusual interrogation.

The subject was a young restaurateur, not a student, not an activist, but a civilian who'd ventured out on foot the morning of June 5 to find red dye and fresh ginger for the celebration of his daughter's birthday. For weeks he'd heard official reports of student protests, how reform movements had been hijacked by political hooligans, capitalist roadsters, and bourgeois liberals. He was still unprepared for the crowds he found in the heart of the city, massive and throbbing. He had a shopping bag in his left hand when he intersected a column of tanks on Chang'an Avenue. The strange spectacle stopped him in the middle of the street. As the tanks approached, his heart pounded with anger, for he sensed some unforgivable bloodshed in the hours behind the tanks, some fastness of smoke and blood, terror and sorrow, now concealed by the staunch, ludicrous forms. The lead tank tried to swerve around him, but he stepped into its path, suddenly determined to die for the sake of a new and holy indignation burning within him—to leave everything behind: his wife, his daughter, the way he'd touched her cheek that morning, smelled her hair, clean-smelling save the faintest scent of sweat, the faintest tang of human oil, and her breath likewise sweet and sour and warm and dainty with life. Yes, he would leave everything behind for this new, soaring sense of justice—

to avenge the mindless murders of the state, the endless humiliations of family and friends, but most of all to appease the sudden and overpowering distaste he felt for a civilization that would send a battery of tanks down a city street the same day he'd chosen to buy gifts for his only child.

He danced with the tanks until they stopped and cut their engines. He climbed onto the first tank and shouted at the driver to forgive his mother. He jumped down and feigned resignation when the engines restarted. He waited for them to grind forward, one second, two seconds, three seconds, then leapt out front and recommenced his grand dance. As he moved with the tanks in a fluid performance, he perceived a glimmer in the sky between the street-side buildings. It was a cool and secret light that spread through him until the rage was gone. He felt like laughing. He was about to laugh when two police officers grabbed his arms and dragged him off the street.

That this anonymous man, this nobody, had gained international fame bothered Luduan. How could an aberration, an accident of emotion, undermine his careful work?

"You've betrayed your people," he told the man in a dim, dripping room of a clandestine prison beneath the city. "Denounce this shameful act, and I may show you mercy."

The tank man laughed, ecstatic in the darkness.

"You will kill me. I will be killed. But you know as I know it was a moment of great strength. That is all."

Luduan breathed through his nostrils.

"We'll have to take care of your family. You've ended their lives, too."

The man was silent. Then he whimpered.

"Your family will answer for your actions," Luduan continued. "It's wrongheaded to think you are strong. Such a belief is foolish and vain. This is the rhetoric I hear from the enemy."

The tank man breathed harshly, grievously.

"You can't stop it," he said. "You are a stupid man to think you can stop it. You can take my children, but your children won't go so easy. You won't be able to control them. They will rise up and destroy you."

Luduan's hand came down like a blade on the man's shoulder, knocking him to the floor. He rarely touched prisoners but had lost his temper.

"I will personally see to the execution of your family," he whispered in the man's ear.

The next morning, after a night of sleeplessness, Luduan followed the shackled man to a soundproof chamber in the center of the prison. He considered using some of his special tools for further interrogation, but decided a quick correction of the mistake was best.

The tank man kneeled on the fresh plastic sheet that had been hurriedly cast over the floor of the room. He didn't say a word as a young guard, no older than twenty, drew a pistol and shot him in the back of the neck.

• • •

STAMER WAITS BEHIND THE bathroom complex at the end of the footbridge. He had his journal inside and was writing so intensely that his mind went to mush. Outside, the words swarm him, abstract and noiseless yet still stinging like mosquitos. *Picnic, lightning. Water, Dorle.* His mind stammers. He considers moving on without them, finding again the dry solace of his lonesome stride. But he doesn't. He looks around the edge of the building and sees them sitting on a bench near the water fountain. He wants to go back and kiss her. He wants to tell her that he can change, that he can be something different than what he's been, but instead he feels a cool, sneaking threat in the air, a turn of fear, the beginning of an alignment of events, like shadows of the trees overlapping each other in quick succession. He can't move because of it.

• • •

THE GINKGO LEAVES SWAM in the city's metallic wind, and their shadows swam in the pools of reddish light that had formed across the campus of Peking University. The redness represented a marriage between the natural sun and the city's industrial smog. Li found the hue alluring while sitting in a painting class he'd elected to take without telling his parents during his second year of college. The redness crept through the classroom windows like the frayed edge of a galaxy. In its sanguine glow, he saw Danyu's face. He saw the flower and emblem of his happiness.

"Many use symbols to wield power," the instructor said. "They take something that's beautiful and meaningful on an individual level and load it with political meaning. They stretch it out. The symbol becomes an umbrella of the state. No longer can an individual find himself in it."

The forty-year-old teacher was slim and striking in appearance. He had thick, wet-looking hair, like the tip of a felt pen. One eye, his right eye, seemed welded to the crook of a severe grin, a permanent grimace. Li would later learn the eye was lame, the result of a three-year prison sentence in the western desert. The teacher now wore a tight-fitting corduroy jacket of dark gray weave that, besides being rare in Beijing, made deft weaponry of his shoulders as he moved around the lectern. His name was Zhou. By that time in the late 1990s, he was steadily gaining, and somewhat enjoying, the ill-fated stardom of dissidence.

Zhou had been a professor of art history and theory before his participation in the Tiananmen Square protests of 1989. As a graduate student, he'd distinguished himself with a series of essays outlining his own aesthetic theory, which he called "strainism." He argued that although a work of art could never transcend the social and political reality in which it was created, it could, through sheer transgressive energy and imagination, represent a new strain in the fabric of society: a unique individuation in the collective system.

After the protests, Zhou was arrested and sent to a labor camp in the arid ranges of northwestern China. He spent three years at a remote quarry loading nameless brown stone into wheelbarrows and pushing it up dusty switchbacks. When once he inquired what the material was for and where it was headed, he was grabbed by the throat and told to shut up. When yet another time he inquired why there was no modern machinery to haul the material and pointed out that the primitive and seemingly useless quarry symbolized the futility of eternal damnation—not progressive reeducation—he was struck in the eye by a rock.

Zhou later returned to the city. He was fortunate his father was a Party member. Through family connections, he was able to return to the university as a teacher of composition. In the mid-nineties, he had made a second reputation for himself by arguing Chinese landscape painters of the Sung Dynasty were the true forerunners of European impressionism. Party officials grew fond of his apparent nationalism, and in time ceded him more autonomy within the university system. His first public art exhibit in the 798 Art District, a colony of galleries that had grown out of decommissioned factories in northeast Beijing, was called "*Guanxi*," or connections. It consisted of a half-dozen abstract paintings done in acrylics. Lines of vibrant color crisscrossed each other over blackness. The thicker the intersections, the more intense the color. In the margins, a few stray strokes had been rendered like pale stems wilting in a black sun. The show sold out. Then another. By the time Li signed up for Zhou's painting class, his teacher was vaguely famous in the world.

" '89," Zhou whispered to Li after class, the day industrial red light had transformed the entire campus into something eerie and beautiful. "Go to the library. Find the student named Fang."

As he spoke, Zhou placed his hand on Li's back in a way that was gentle and sensual.

"You are a talented student. I can tell by the economy of your sketches. You are hungry for the truth."

The library was empty. There was no student named Fang, at least not at the tables where Li asked around. But there was a book lying on a vacant table with the same name embossed in the spine. It was a history book about martial arts in the Han Dynasty. Between the cover and first page was a note containing the title of another book, *Ch'an*. When Li made an inquiry into its whereabouts, the librarian on duty, a short, soft-edged woman, lowered her eyes and whispered, " '89," then slid him a sheet of paper on which she'd written the location of the second book. He followed the instructions into the tall, musty stacks of Chinese history. There was no one else among the shelves. He noticed the black apparatus of a surveillance camera in the high corner of the ceiling, a single eyeball in what he knew was a much more complex system of technological omnipresence. He found the book. It was an obscure aesthetics treatise written in the last days of the Sung Dynasty. Inside was a key to a locker in the school's athletic complex.

By the time Li reached the locker room, it, too, was devoid of students, as though his pursuit had precluded any possibility of companionship. Inside the locker was a dossier. The first thing Li saw was a black-and-white photograph of his father. The accompanying text was a report, presumably compiled by Zhou, detailing the Tiananmen Square protest and Luduan's involvement in the ensuing crackdown.

"Are there others?" Li asked his professor that same evening. He'd found him in his office, dark except the humming blue light of a computer. "Am I the only one?"

"There are many others. We don't meet in public."

"How do you know these things about my father?"

"We follow our enemies. We have done this for years."

Zhou flipped on a lamp then stood up.

"You must know what you see here can never be revealed to others. These are matters of life and death."

He walked over to Li and put his hand on his shoulder. His fingers slid down Li's arm leaving a warm tingle. The teacher then took the dossier from the student's trembling hand.

"When you are ready, we will talk about the next step."

That night, ignoring his other studies—reams of mathematical formulae, principles of civil engineering—Li took a fresh piece of willow charcoal and sketched his father. His strokes, like lashes, lifted the teeth of the paper. His crosshatches dug into the surface and blackened his knuckles. He pried and ripped at the paper until his father stared back at him, startled him with his cruelty.

"The eyebrows are so fierce," Zhou commented the next day while examining the work. "He is a fiend, isn't he?"

Li remained quiet, still frightened by the sketch, the scratches in the paper, the shading of the face, the dossier in the locker.

"You did this from memory? No modeling?"

Li nodded.

"Excellent economy."

Before Li could turn away, Zhou grabbed his arm.

"Remember, the enemy is unmerciful, so we must be unmerciful."

● ● ●

LI CAN'T RECALL WHAT time the hike began. The estrangement of the hours wears his thoughts down to isolated images. Fallen branches on the forest floor. Pebbles stuck in the tread of his shoe. She is beautiful, he is thinking now, watching Dorle sip water from a sweating plastic bottle she uncovered from her fanny pack. Stamer must return, he thinks. He wouldn't be a coward to leave us, would he? What if he doesn't come back? What will you tell her?

The river breaks on the boulders in continuous revolution. Each spray is a revision of the past, an assertion of the present.

"I never believed in gods," Li tells her. "In China, religions are restricted. But I read once of Guanyin, the Buddhist goddess of mercy.

I thought if something greater than us existed, it would be this thing, this creature not like us in our narrow ways, but much bigger and open to all the mistakes we make. What a beautiful idea it is."

Dorle puts the bottle back in her fanny pack. Zips it shut. Her eyes fall on the Merced.

"I've never been religious either. The first time I prayed was the first night I spent in jail—"

She stops herself, trying to choke the revelation before it rises too high in the air. Li is motionless.

"Sorry, that's another story. But praying came easy to me. No one ever taught me how to do it, but that night, I just did it." Her voice thickens. "I was so down in life, so sick of myself. I had nowhere else to go."

Suddenly she laughs out—the kind of laughter that cracks and bruises the throat. Li wonders if she's hysterical. He remembers Danyu laughing the same way whenever she sensed danger.

"I didn't even believe in God. Still don't. But I prayed that night. All I could do was throw myself into the crazy idea that someone or something out there could save me. I opened myself up to the possibility, and it was so powerful. This feeling of grace overwhelmed me. It unlocked me. I cried all through the night. You know what it was, don't you?"

Li nods.

"Mercy," she says. "Forgiveness washing over me like this river."

• • •

LI HAD NO MERCY as a young breakthrough artist. His nights were ruled by solitary rage. He tore into Danyu whenever making love. He bit and slapped her, pulled her hair. She cried in pain and pleasure, baffled by the new hell in her lover's face. She took it all until their naked bodies lay tangled together like flowers of clay and ash.

"I can't go home again," he told her the same week he sketched his father. "We will live in the art district. I will make enough money selling my work."

"Won't you finish school?" she asked, remembering her mother's admonitions. *An honorable man must provide his own apartment, a car, and a child.* "What if your work does not sell?"

Li took off his glasses and rubbed his eyes.

"Do you love me, Danyu?"

"I do, but I am worried."

"Don't worry. You are my *yinghua*. I will make you happy."

Their first apartment was a rancid studio space above a busy and smoky restaurant known for its roasted duck. Art dealers had made other buildings on the street world-famous, but the restaurant owners, old-school Maoists, had resisted gentrification. They let their brick walls stand proudly in a translucent coat of grease. Black smoke spewed from misshapen vents. Li hated it. Danyu was indifferent. It reminded her of their old neighborhood near Tiananmen Square.

Some nights Li rose in the toxic shadows of the city and locked himself in the bathroom with his paints and canvas. For ventilation, he'd prop open the small, mold-splotched window. The city's metallic air would creep inside and ring his nerves into an almost unbearable tinnitus. He'd clench his mouth, breathe through his nose, and between the narrow walls, the sink and the toilet, he'd work in a frenzy. He'd work like he'd thrown a wedge in time and had to hurry before the universe reclaimed its secrets. At first, he'd attack his canvas with impasto and knife cuts, building and tearing the texture simultaneously. Then he'd stalk wild strains of music in thick, panting brushstrokes, over and over, dabbing and stroking, stroking and fanning. Last to come were the glazes of his thin brushes, as exquisite as the seconds after orgasm, when love breaks from its swollen chains and quivers with wonder. He knew it was this heightened brushwork that could strike something new into existence, this delicate breath of color both creating and revealing the world. He felt there was an exact moment when he could turn the old values of the world upside down—in a single flourish subvert the old and present the new.

It was how he painted "The Red Door." He'd built the drab walls of the hutong with earthy grays and browns and gleams of yellow. For the door itself, embedded in the wall, he'd first lain purplish shadows, like a ravished veil hanging from the doorjambs. Over this veil his vermillion asserted itself. It came from his brush like pure fire. His red covered the purple until the door glowed in defiance of the walls that braced it. Li worked on the painting until dawn, emerging from the bathroom like a war refugee, glasses off, hair splattered with red paint.

"What is it?" Danyu asked. "You are scaring me."

"I have to go to the university," he answered. "I have to go now."

He hurried to his teacher's office. Zhou's lame eye twitched as he took the painting from Li's hand and set it on a chair near an open window.

"This is the beginning," Zhou said. "I want you to look at your work and tell me what you see."

Li stepped up to his own creation. In the morning light of the window, the painting burned like a dream of heaven he once had.

"I see—"

He stopped. Some smoldering mauve color seeped through the red door like smoke. The hue was cool like the back of Danyu's neck. He took a step back, suddenly afraid to open the door.

"I'll tell you what I see," Zhou said, stepping directly behind his student.

Li felt Zhou's hands come up and rest on his arms. He felt Zhou's breath in his ear. For the first time, he thought his teacher might desire him.

"I see the beginning of the end of the Party."

Weeks passed. As Li began meeting with other students in secret, Danyu was enveloped by a sense of doom. She didn't know where Li was going after class each day. She didn't know what kept him out into the late hours of the night, the early hours of the morning, but she knew their lives had veered sharply away from one another. When she was alone in the apartment, listening to the racket in the restaurant below, cooks shouting at each other, patrons, drunk on rice wine, bellowing with laughter, she would lay prostrate on their bed and weep into her hands. She would remember those nights as children playing on the shores of the western lakes, watching the colored lanterns float on the water like wishes. Li had been so shy as a child, so gentle. And now his paintings, stacked in the corner, offered her something monstrous and defiant, a violent aberration of the man she'd known. She couldn't escape the feeling that in those paintings lay her own ruin.

Zhou called their secret meeting place Xanadu. It was no more than an underground tunnel Mao had built during the Cold War. It stretched for miles under the city, and the government still used part of it for transporting clandestine prisoners. Zhou had done enough digging to locate an abandoned section accessible by a single door at the end of a derelict hutong in the depths of the old city. When students first met in the dripping, rat-squeaking recesses of Xanadu, they assumed they were in some sort of aqueduct. They didn't know they were actually inside the black heart of the enemy.

"*This* is our Temple of Heaven," Zhou proclaimed their first meeting. "It is a temple of the imagination, of desire, and the power of self over the state. Power does not lie with Party officials. It does not lie with the Committee members. It lies with us, the artists. Only artists can provide what China needs. We can change the People's minds. We have power over perception."

Li was the youngest artist of the group, but the other men (Zhou had not recruited a single woman) recognized he was the favored one and deferred to him as they would a lieutenant.

"What will we do?" Li asked.

Zhou's grin sharpened nefariously.

"We will do what we always do. We will paint!"

It began as graffiti: dissident slogans from the Tiananmen Square protests more than a decade earlier now wielded in the new millennium with new force, lavishly painted on any building they could access at night, in the art district, the tech districts—which were sharply lit and hard to penetrate—and soon enough in the old city itself, in the modernized ruins of their shared heritage. Along with written characters appeared glorious murals: black-haired students astride fire-breathing dragons and tigers, the human faces concealed by lashes of red paint. Some of the figures were left half-finished in the dawn-light, as if composed by vandal ghosts. City authorities picked up on the patterns, but the Ministry of State Security wasn't involved until an obscene balloon landed in the middle of Tiananmen Square. One morning it floated down like a discarded party favor, touched the ground lightly—Mao's inflated, three-dimensional head fashioned on the plump and fatuous body of a skinned duck.

When Luduan was notified, he rushed to the site. His first reaction was nausea from the irony. Then he grew angry. He tottered from side to side, searching the air for a source of the derision. Finding none, he stormed back into his office and ordered his inferiors to check surrounding buildings, anywhere of significant height. It was one of those inferiors who informed him of the greater desecration taking place throughout the city. The main suspects, he reported, were university students, specifically art students.

• • •

WE HAVE TO CONFRONT these feelings, Stamer thinks. We have to confront this doom. We can challenge it. We can stand up, walk over, and punch it in the face. Less. Than. All. Cannot. Satisfy. Man.

But this woman deserves more than man. More than two briefcases stuffed with cash. Can you hear me, Sparky? Kristopher? How about you, Forster, you grand fuck?

God, help me. I'm not made for this. I'm not equipped for this. I don't know how to love people.

• • •

BEIJING'S NEWEST HIPSTERS LAUGHED at the stern and silent man darting in and out of art galleries in the spring of 2005. They didn't know he was one of the most trusted and most ruthless agents of the Party's intelligence arm. He looked severe, reeking of injury and desperation. They didn't know he was not himself that night, that what was severe in him, as sharp as a Tang sword, was his keening pride. They dismissed him as senile when he cut in front of a huge line in front of 798's newest gallery, The Red Door.

The wordless man walked from exhibit to exhibit, with an intense focus that could have been mistaken for aesthetic appreciation. The curators inside did mistake him for a serious critic, a wealthy buyer. They bowed politely when he dismissed them with a wave of his hand. Then he came to the eponymous painting at the end of an arcade, the painting that had inspired the new gallery and lifted a tight clan of Peking University students into stratospheric fame. He slowly inhaled as he received the image.

"Are you all right?" one of the curators asked.

Luduan exhaled and looked at the inquirer, who was young and raffish like a prince. He felt nothing but contempt. He felt no sympathy for the young man or his generation. He wanted them destroyed. When he turned back to the painting, his eyes winced at the color. The red door was so vivid. Too vivid. It was a statement against him; he was sure of it. And the walls. He knew those walls. He knew that place in the hutong. But not the door. Never in his life had he seen the door. Even before asking for the artist's name, he somehow knew his own son had created it.

• • •

STAMER WALKS BACK TO the bridge and flies up the steps with surprising ease, as though lifted by the mere thought of ascension.

Li sees him and stands with an overjoyed expression on his face. Dorle stands just as Stamer reaches her. He reels her on the haunted air and brings his lips to hers. The kiss is abrupt and utterly imperfect but also wet and hot and mutually vital. Dorle relaxes enough to adjust, enough to feel the blood spiking in her body.

Birds break from the trees. The bridge's onlookers twitter in and out of time. At the bottom of the falls, in that locus of pressure and erasure, a rainbow appears. The colors tremble, then fade.

PART THREE

H is breath stinks. It's the stink of stress. The stink of worry that lives way down in the stomach and drifts up the esophagus in acidic waves. It's the stink of a man who has a mortgage back in the suburbs, a wife, two children, the weight of the unknown, every menacing variable working against him all the time. It's the stink of a man who has left behind some haven of comfort, some better time in the past that he now thinks of bitterly. It's the stink of a man who no longer finds joy in his work, who no longer sees a brighter future, who no longer can figure out a way to die with dignity when the time comes.

It's the breath of National Park Service Ranger Randy McFall as he stands near a posted fork in the Mist Trail checking permits for excursions up Half Dome.

Earlier in the day, during the bus ride up the valley, Gina's bus (he's so sick of her tirades), he told a man sitting next to him about lightning deaths on the malformed peak, if for no other reason than to elicit a thrill, to share with the stranger the power of some arcane and awful conspiracy against the dead. But the man rejected his advances, and Randy felt his feeble excitement for the day die before ever being born, relapsing into dullness, the thick reek of his own breath.

There was a time for him when Half Dome was a symbol of life's grandeur. He remembers how excited he used to get coming to the park. It was when he was still teaching elementary school in Fresno, before the house, when the kids were young and his wife, Caroline, ate breakfast with him every morning. Raisin Bran and toast. Coffee and orange juice. He can taste the juice now, the wild, ferric tang of it, the clink of glass on wood, her cheek down-soft as he kisses her goodbye. He can see it now. One last glance in the children's room. They're sleeping so purely, so untroubled. Then the car downstairs in the covered parking stall, a green Ford Taurus sleeping over the apartment number painted on the asphalt. Driving away, he feels like a man with purpose, as solid and direct as the steering wheel he turns with his hand. The park comes later. Caroline wants a house. He needs the extra income in the summer. They'll visit him on the weekends, but he sets out alone. He hasn't been to the park since a child, and Yosemite Valley takes his breath away. The cliffs are gilded curtains opening on a stage of luscious green, as ripe as anything he has ever seen. The water runs through it all like a serpentine spirit, from the high falls to the deep pools of the river, constantly washing and waking the senses. The peaks above hold the secrets of the water. He wants to go there. He wants to climb as a man with ultimate purpose, with the greatest devotion—

He still keeps the collected writings of John Muir in his daypack. But the language has failed him. Or he has failed the language. He doesn't know which—

The promise of adulthood erodes over the years. He goes on to teach high school, even coaches a division-winning basketball team. He and his wife buy a respectable home with two stories and a three-car garage, all of which he can barely afford on his salary. The mortgage allows his children to grow into moody, vindictive teenagers, who wield an arsenal of gadgetry that frightens him. Caroline starts sleeping in late every morning. He sees her only in the evenings, their dinners a disconsolate twilight in which they fumble toward whatever rubbery alien food he or she microwaved from the freezer. Everything becomes expedient, twinged with desperation. They fight over the children, their shared future, the gauntlet of higher education. They fight over money. Some fights progress into shouting and door-slamming. They go to bed early, drained of all feeling for each other, sullen shells adrift in the magenta light pollution of suburbia.

The park is his escape each summer. The family visits less and less, and he starts spending time with the younger temps in the camps. He hikes and climbs and enjoys their nightly parties. He writes fewer citations and drinks more beer. He flirts with the young women. The prospect of an affair crosses his mind more than once. He waits for someone to make a move, anyone. But no one ever does. He concludes he's no longer desirable, or maybe was never desirable. When he's reprimanded by his supervisor for being too lenient, he realizes he is alone in the world. He breaks ties with the friends he's made in the camps and begins walking the trails by himself. Each season, he grows more and more isolated. He becomes the odd and lonesome figure others laugh about when he's not around.

The park has its consolations, though. He immerses himself in the forest, in the gloomy silence of the tall pines, in the sunny oaks along the river. He studies the bird calls that tinkle and drip from the trees. He studies wildflowers and native shrubs. The alpine asters are his favorite showing. They're small and dainty, and the way they nod with happiness reminds him of his children when they were young. But their charms and the greater charms of nature fade. He knows something in him has changed when the solitude of an empty trail or a secret glen no longer enchants him. His mind poisons what were sacred places. They begin to frighten him. Each season, there's an uptick of tourist deaths, more fatalities on the peaks and in the river. The park turns from a place of tranquility, of stable forms secured by summer light, into a place of chaos and desolation, of unrecognizable forms ruled by accident and nothing more.

Later, he assumes patrol duties on the lower Mist Trail, a move that rejuvenates him for a time. The mist keeps his face fresh and clean. The crowds keep his thoughts entertained. He begins craving contact with strangers. The need intensifies. It's the corollary of his fear. He offers support to the sick and old, water to the thirsting, advice to the confused or lost, knowledge to the eager. But as much as he likes helping people, it isn't enough. He begins craving confrontation. He begins stalking infractions like a cougar, pouncing on the smoker, the swimmer, the toe-dipper—any fool with the wrong permit for a given activity. His citations pour down in torrents of reproach. Visitors are startled. Some dismiss his attitude as overreaction. Others, especially those new to the mountains, suspect obvious deficiencies within themselves. He punishes them. He embarrasses them.

And today is no different. He decides to return to the bridge just as a peculiar trio approaches the fork in the trail. A blond woman in a camouflage hat. A Chinese man wearing glasses. And another man... the man from the bus.

Rage grips Randy McFall. He's simultaneously confused, stymied by something akin to shame, the disappointment of having failed to win the man's affection or even some small acknowledgement of his own authority. The injury burns and breaches the air with uncertain heat. He sees the man has made friends, attractive friends, and they're enjoying each other's company. Resentment barks in his brain. Bites. He takes a step back, at a loss for words. The man's face rises in passing, the gray eyes searching, narrowing. Then the slightest smile. Not even a smile. The phantom of a smile. The ghost of a feeling. The hope attached to movement. Upward mobility. A better day. A better life.

"How y'all doing today?" the ranger asks, instantly appalled by his own voice.

He feels ridiculous in front of them.

"We're well. Thank you, sir," Li nods kindly.

But it's not enough. Randy McFall slips into a gray panic. The river is pounding his temples. He's trying desperately to surface, to triumph.

"If you're going up the falls, be careful up top. It's slippery. Don't even think about going in the water."

His warning falls short. Suddenly he's aware of the insuperable thickness of the trail, the dark, moist earth, padded between stones, on this north-facing side of the canyon.

"I'll keep my eyes on you!" he shouts.

But they're already ahead of him. He snorts in contempt. He decides he'll stay at the post for another hour.

• • •

STAMER CAN'T QUITE PLACE the ranger's look. He remembers their discussion on the bus, the description of lightning on human flesh. But any fear then is now gone. Dorle's kiss has dispatched it. He feels invincible. The fresh memory of her lips mingles with the damp smells of the forest and the soft birdcalls dispelling stone. Seeing the ranger again, he feels not a tinge of fear or guilt—just ecstatic silliness.

Now he touches her back, palpitations, rivets of flesh. He realizes he hasn't been this far on the trail. He's spent most of his time down in the valley. He's a tourist; he knows this now. The trail is curving back toward that spectacular cataract that fixes the whole scene. In a flash he sees the ranger's absurdity, that strangeness marking the way, but other signs, too. He sees a different face, back in Vegas, Forster's face. Quizzical eyes dancing upon fate.

• • •

THEY MOVED TO VEGAS together in the late 1990s. The superannuated piousness of Salt Lake City had worn them out, curtailed their disposable income. Vegas was the antithesis of a holy city. It had no past. It had no reason for existence. It offered grandeur without history, glamour without morality.

They each found their own place as close to the Strip as possible. In their first months there, while Forster was searching for a new office, Stamer was exploring the massive casinos that sprouted from the earth in fantastic shapes and colors. He grew fascinated with the mock landmarks: the pyramids, the towers. Their mimicry was bombastic. Great sarcastic sphinxes sailing across the desert sand, winking at centuries of slavery. The model cities were his favorite, though. He could open a door and find himself in a microcosm of all human achievement, everything condensed, distilled for entertainment, like the elaborate habitat of a human zoo. His first time inside New York, New York, he

tried to find the roller coaster but got lost in a maze of simulacra: streets
and shops and windows and signs all imitating some quaint precinct
of Manhattan. He ordered a roast beef sandwich from a corner deli.
Standing beneath its green-and-white-striped awning, he believed, for
a moment, that he was in the greatest metropolis in the world. Then his
eyes alighted on a rack of cheap souvenirs on the other side of the street.
The trinkets and knickknacks were advertising not New York City itself,
but the New York City of some metamorphic commercial burlesque:
models of models manufactured in China. He walked around, sandwich in hand, gazing down the fabulous avenues. Suddenly the cars of
the roller coaster thundered overhead. He followed the noise to a set of
stairs, which led to a catwalk over the ersatz city. Again, looking down
on the immense and intricate arcades, he perceived something akin
to infinity. It will never end, he thought, and the thought delighted
him—as though he, too, could create life from life and never die.

Forster had talked Stamer into severing all ties with Squeals &
Anderson. The two men would incorporate a new firm in Nevada.
Forster had already chosen a name: AmerzWest Capital Corp. It
sounded dull and mundane to Stamer, especially knowing his friend's
proclivity for the extravagant, but Forster maintained they needed a
name that was basic and sterile, stripped of all sex appeal, a name that
would even bore the S.E.C. Originally, the men were to be equal partners, with equal equity and distribution of profits, but the day they
filed with the state, Stamer urged his friend to take a majority stake.
He didn't know exactly why. A strong yet mysterious instinct told
him he would be better off as a minority partner. Forster agreed and
declared himself chief executive officer and president of the board.
Stamer became executive vice president of operations and also took
a position on the board. To fill the position of chief financial officer,
Forster hired a retired moneyman he'd met at the Flamingo. His name
was Karl. Stamer thought he looked like a holdout from the city's
chintzy mafia era. He had silver, slick-combed hair at the temples,
underscoring a much whiter, teetering crest of hair above. His fore-

head was extrusive, reddened and shiny. His eyes, set in a long, wrinkled face, were dull green and watery. He wore stiff, pin-striped suits, or smoky, checkered sweaters with slacks. And fat rings on his hands. And gold chains around his neck. He must have been pushing seventy, and to Stamer, he came off as being bitter in a feeble way—spoiled, whining, ratlike.

The partners spent their first years in Vegas updating their licensure, refiling with every requisite agency, and formulating new holdings as quickly as possible. Forster had decided long ago that trading equities and bonds was a losing game. He came to detest traders themselves as parasites, unable to create and sustain lasting worth. True value, he argued, required tangible assets, property he could see and touch and embrace, things in themselves existing not independent of market value—that constant euphoric flux he now distrusted—but beneath it. His new idea of wealth rested on a vague notion of bedrock, of some indisputable worth upon which, he thought, everything else was built. To this end, real estate became his game. Real estate could never depreciate, he proclaimed.

AmerzWest Capital Corp.'s first project would be its greatest project, though the partners didn't know it at the time. City officials were salivating for redevelopment projects in older districts of the city that lagged behind the Strip's predominant appeal. One such blighted area was called Custer Square. In the city's short life, it had once been the center of municipal operations. It had once, in a bouquet of Southwest-style buildings, been the pink, florid heart of the desert city. But as casinos rose over time, only a few miles away, Custer Square fell into the abortive shadows of history, deserted by those who loved it most. Graffiti crawled higher and higher up the sides of its buildings. Abandoned scaffolding clattered and choked its windows. The park in the middle of the square, which had been an emblem of civility and public improvement, became a refuge for the homeless, the junky, the dealer, the prostitute, the john, the pimp—all the city's disgorged destitute and desperate.

It was only with the advent of the new millennium that local policy hounds turned their attention to the forsaken square. During the last election cycle of the twentieth century, city council candidates exploited the growing resentment of their citizenry, a bourgeoning disillusionment with the faux Disneyland the city had become. A fervid campaign began to salvage and restore Custer's honor. Candidates pledged unimpeded progress toward a redevelopment district: a private-public partnership that would furnish the city with a sense of tradition, a proud historical legacy devoid of casinos and mafia chiefs, a made-up history of brave pioneers, rugged individuals, and devoted public servants. Candidates who fully embraced the plan were swept into office. At public meetings afterwards, TV reporters questioned the status of the project, impassioned, zealous, promising viewers their voices were still important, that they, the media, would not let the issue die. Reporters competed with each other over whom offered more accountability. The project would go forward at all costs, they said. But who among them, in the leadership, in the viewership, had the vision and wherewithal to save a rotten urban core?

Stamer knew Forster was interested even before his partner officially announced that AmerzWest Capital Corp. would be applying for redevelopment funding at Custer Square. Several other developers and firms were interested as well, but Forster was confident he had the edge. The city was offering not only tax abatements, but actual cash payments to the successful applicant. To be funded by projected increases in tax revenue in the redeveloped zone, the payments would be meted out over a twenty-year schedule and would increase with time. The last payment itself, on the twentieth year, would total $7.2 million, according to the development agreement. The only contractual stipulation the city made was the developer add at least thirty thousand square feet of new commercial space and maintain tenant occupancy of at least 80 percent. The city was selling Custer Square as a prime location for an outdoor mall, a unique, walkable retail space with historic charm and close proximity to the Strip. Forster, however, had another vision, and he began courting city council members with his plans and declamations.

Stamer imagined how his friend would reveal the Bengal Tower to those reactionary faces. Like a magician sweeping back his cape? Or like a steely tactician, building consensus slowly, painfully, before giving up the smallest detail? What the city really needed, Forster began to argue, was not something antithetical to the Strip, but something that could extend the Strip's unquestionable success to its quarters. In his vision, a handful of the Custer buildings would be preserved for niche retailers and restaurants, but the old city hall, that shabby plastered front that was the defining showpiece of the square, would have to go. In its place, a new kind of casino would rise, an establishment that would rival, and capitalize on, the glitz and glamor of the Strip, but would also revitalize nongaming industry, diversify the local economy, and attract the biggest and brightest talent from around the globe. It would be the first of its kind: a luxury hotel and casino that doubled as an office tower and business center. Imagine the snap and sizzle of the casino floor, the fall of dice and cards, the shuffle of chips across the tables, the ringing slot machines all washed in cool white lighting. Then imagine below the casino floor, at the basement level, a vast network of business conference rooms, fiber-optic telecom hubs, and opulent lobbies overflowing with fine art and exotic plants and leather lounge chairs. On the other side of the tower, proportionate to the hotel suites, office suites would be clustered together in a great buzzing honeycomb.

This is how Forster sold the project: the ultimate combination of work and play. What he needed to materialize the vision, brandishing MOUs from eager investors, was not merely a design variance, but a whole new zoning category created solely for the purpose of the Bengal Tower, a zoning district that would blend tourist commercial and office commercial. Such a distinction would require an amendment to existing code.

"Why call it the Bengal?" asked council chair Robert Kip during his first private meeting with Forster.

"Easy. Asia. This city's been so focused on Western culture that we've neglected our key partnership for the future. We all know growth in this century will come from China and India. Why shut ourselves out? Their citizens don't want to see our relics. We've worn 'em out. We've stretched 'em as far as they'll go. They want to see themselves in our city. This is the greatest city in the world. Why the Bengal? I believe it will build a path right back to the Orient. With the right attraction, the right lure, the tiger will come to us."

In a matter of weeks, Forster had turned half the city board. He needed one more vote to seal a majority. But the remaining council members were obstinate. Details of Forster's plan had leaked out from the private meetings, and the press pounced on what they viewed as a blatant hijacking of their own idealistic campaign. Columnists and correspondents called in contrarian policy buffs for back up, most of them urban planning professors from local colleges, all of them denouncing any casino at Custer Square as a probable failure and colossal waste of taxpayer money. Such technical explanatory journalism was followed by scathing editorials accusing city members of bowing to big money and selling out the very voters who'd guaranteed their positions. Populist anger grew. There were threats of recall. Forster revisited those members whom he'd already persuaded. He reassured them the outrage was spurious and transitory. He reassured them their seats were safe and promised as much funding as possible for reelection. Voters would soon recognize the economic benefits of the project, he told them. Custer Square would become something great and worthy of their admiration.

At the same time, Forster knew some members were capitalizing on the controversy. Their opposition to the deal was almost as theatrical and grandiose as the proposal itself. All he needed was one more vote, one more member on his side, but he realized his powers of persuasion were limited against the frenzied moral superiority of a snowballing press campaign. What he needed, really, was a weak link, someone he could turn.

When the night of the vote finally came, all Stamer knew was that Forster had talked to Karl, their new CFO, and that Karl had contacted one of his old associates. Like everyone else, Stamer was surprised when council member John Belchek, who, days before, had eviscerated the project on a popular talk show, retracted his entire statement. In what was the most publicized, well-attended civic meeting in city history, Belchek threw his full support behind the Bengal Tower.

● ● ●

THEY ENTER A TUNNEL hollowed out in the side of the mountain. There's an archaic wetness on the granite floor, an old, particulate moisture. It reminds Dorle of the smell of the cellar in her childhood home, its gritted must. But here, on the trail, the smell is cleaner, like a stone altar. She's thinking of her daughter. She's not thinking of Stamer or their kiss on the bridge, though the kiss opened up something inside her. A sprout. A budding awareness. Dora hates me, she thinks. She loves her father, and she hates me.

Stamer catches Li's face at the exit of the tunnel. A shaded, sighing look turning toward light. Li stops, as if in warning, then dissolves into the open. Stamer lets Dorle pass in front of him. Her shoes scrape on the stone and then she's off into the light as well. Before following, Stamer feels the inside of the cavity with his hand, the granite cool and smoothed by so much passing. He's thinking of another woman he almost loved. Not Kimberly. Not the kiss on the bridge. It was in Vegas. Her body was cool and smooth and hard like this stone.

● ● ●

HE MET GRESHEN AT the opening of the Bengal Tower in the spring of 2002. Construction of the building had been delayed after the terrorist attacks of September 11th. Forster brought on a new security team.

He vowed to take no chances—protecting what he called the sacred covenant between man and investor—nor risk the beneficence of the taxpayer.

"It's not religious at all," he told Stamer the week they watched the towers collapse on national television. "No one attacks because of their religion or another person's religion. That's such a poor excuse. They attack us because they can't compete. Our system scares them. I've seen it in their eyes during my travels. They're terrified of me. And they should be terrified. We'll devour them."

Forster siphoned off security experts from Salt Lake City who'd come to prominence during the 2002 Winter Olympic Games. The security/surveillance industry had skyrocketed overnight, and Forster had to pay a premium for the experts. Looking over his plans and manifests, they recommended a heightened security presence at all major entrances during construction, and increased monitoring of all freight and delivery to the site. Furthermore, subcontractors were subjected to background checks. Most complied. Those who refused were let go. When Forster presented plans for a grand opening on the first day of spring, his consultants recommended thrice the amount of security personnel, rigorous vetting of any media outlets covering the event, and an inviolate guest list.

Greshen was not on the guest list the night of the grand opening. Stamer was touring the casino floor with a handful of print reporters when he saw her sitting alone on a scarlet-topped barstool in a sapphire-lit cabaret lounge.

"Excuse me," he told the group of reporters, many of them twenty-something interns with spotty beards and chic glasses, all of them united in their defiant impish posture not yet accountable to the inevitable decline of their industry.

As Stamer walked toward the woman, he saw two smoking, gaping holes in the thick cubic stratum of New York City. He remembered his dream of the blind, screaming device in his hand.

"I'm sorry, I'm gonna have to ask for your invitation, ma'am."

She was smoking a plastic-tipped cigarette while holding a half-empty martini glass in her other hand.

"Oh, really?" she asked, tilting her head with a cool jaunt.

Stamer recalled the similar face of a woman in his old bank. Blond hair spilling from a seamless mold. The woman before him was a product of the same careful tooling. He could see how the bleached layered hair was carefully needled along the perimeter of the scalp. The head itself was sculptural, yet of a common cast, as if mass-produced, with sparkling green eyes and hot-red lips painted for a glossy finish. On the stool her lanky body made a coherent set piece, wrapped tightly in a black satin dress. Even the fleshy edges of her figure were burnished like faux marble.

"Do you have one, an invitation? I know it seems like we're open, but the gathering tonight is actually a private function."

She smiled knowingly and sipped her martini, then pivoted her head to scan the empty lounge. A few men, stragglers, ties loosened, had escaped the festivities; the casino floor was tinkling with their gradual exploration.

"You would turn away a potential customer the day before opening to the public?" she asked. "It seems to me the only invitation I need is the fact your security goons let me in. Perhaps it's because I know every man here."

Her eyes descended with a slanted sharpness, silent and ferocious.

"Almost every man," she said.

Stamer took her to one of five executive suites on the twenty-sixth floor. She undressed quickly, mechanically. He was still dressed and standing beside the bed when she bent down and found his cock with her mouth. He held the back of her head as she pumped him into hardness. Then he took off his pants and bent her over the bed. He spanked her and penetrated her at the same time. She squealed. He groaned and hissed. Her reddened butt cheek felt like an unpeeled orange in his grip. It quivered, the only part of her she let loose. He could feel the rest of her burnished body maintaining its rigidity, clicking in doll-like machinations. The back rolling rhythmically. The blonde hair snapping against the neck. Even her moans, after the initial squeal, became constant and predictable, as if set to a hidden timer. This made him angry. He spanked her harder, fucked her faster. But the emitted sounds remained the same. He groped his way around the body and cupped the breasts with his hands. These, too, he was surprised to find, were consistent with the main, taut and limited in their movement.

"Fuck!" he shouted.

Her eyes. He longed to see her eyes, how they'd be different. But before he could flip her over, his own body bucked in sharp rebuke. He pulled out, spraying himself across her knuckled spine.

She was quiet at first, motionless, perceiving the new wetness on her exterior.

"Well, that was rather quick," she said.

He walked to the bathroom and got two towels. He mopped up his groin with one and threw the other on the bed.

"A little help?" she said. "I gotta get going. I shouldn't be up here."

He dressed as quickly as she had undressed. He didn't look at her as she maneuvered around the bed trying to clean herself.

"Thanks," he said.

His exit, the click of the door in place, sealed their tacit agreement. He would provide her access to the lifestyle, the market for which she was designed. In return, she would not demand remittance. She would not charge him for services rendered as she had charged almost every other man.

• • •

"WHY ARE YOU LAGGING so far behind?" he hears Dorle ask him, sunlight breaking against his eyes, a glissando of yellow hues.

"I..."

His eyes readjust to the gray dimensions of the canyon. Dorle and Li have stepped off the trail to let others pass. They stand patiently on

an inadvertent overlook, a small raw point in the slope split by a lone
pine. Stamer can see the mists beyond their heads. The falls resume a
steady sonic presence.

"Sorry, I was distracted by the cave."

Dorle smiles. Her face is moistly relaxed, wholly flushed and hale,
with a newfound confidence Stamer finds attractive and troubling. He
can see a train of people winding up the right field of his vision. Actually, two trains of people: one going up and one coming down the slick
stone steps, gliding beside one another on invisible tracks. The trail
disappears in the buckled canyon between there and where they stand.
How far? he thinks. What more is there to tell?

• • •

THE DAY STAMER RETURNED from his business trip to China was the day
his relationship with Greshen ended.

He'd traveled with an insouciant contingent of state tourism officials and economic development consultants. Their mission, always,
was to attract foreign investment, new ventures, new visitors. Specifically, the state wanted not only more Chinese interest in Nevada
minerals, geothermal and solar energy projects, but to expand marketing and advertising channels in Beijing. Las Vegas, they declaimed, was
a world-class destination worthy of a mutually beneficial partnership
between the Chinese government and the state government of Nevada.
The pitch went like this: imagine cheap and easy access to Nevada's
abundant copper supply, its endless underground drift of gold, and
then imagine exclusive bidding rights, long-term supply agreements,
and a regulatory environment conducive to export.

"All we ask in return is access to the single largest growing demo-
graphic on the face of the planet—your citizens, Mr. Fang."

Stamer had been tasked with courting Party operatives in the
propaganda department, along with a retinue of state journalists and
telecom executives. Mr. Fang hailed from the propaganda department

and was acting head of the consort that had lured Stamer midafternoon to a famous Peking duck restaurant at the end of a crumbling alley. He was a short, shiny-cheeked man with a matching bald head and glasses. He wore a treacly, peach-colored shirt that Stamer found abhorrent. When Stamer ordered coffee, an emaciated waiter, so thin and quiet in contrast, told him they only had tea.

"With our resources," Stamer continued, "you could bring mainland China into the twenty-first century. You could run wire all the way to Afghanistan."

"Your offer is very attractive to my colleagues in rural development. But you know that we are limited in our tourism campaigns, and all of these are internal for our own heritage sites. We reciprocate with other nations in allowing access to our travel offices and secretaries, if they do likewise with our most valued destinations. But I don't think we can give you what you want, which is a campaign in the city. The urban departments don't care about your copper as you think. And our urban citizens don't care about your recreation. The world has called them a middle class without a brain, without political rights. 'Prosperity without liberty.' But this is a great falsehood. Our citizens care deeply about their culture and the well-being of others. I believe many would be offended to visit such a place as your Bengal Tower and its false tributes. I've read the reviews—very impressive, but for Westerners, not for the Chinese."

The other men in the group were silent. It was clear that Mr. Fang had received his orders and would grant Nevada no special advantage in the Party-controlled marketplace of images and influence. Stamer finished his tea and left amicably. But his inner mood matched the fuming black smoke billowing from the kitchen vents outside the restaurant. He trudged along a crooked alleyway and back into a crowded street. He lost his footing and was swept away in a current of hustling, pole-thin people. They reminded him of the coal miners and iron workers from his youth in Pennsylvania. Except this was China. The country had a restless energy he hadn't experienced anywhere else in the world. It was frantic but buoyant. It carried him on the rivers of people until a small boy in a baseball cap grabbed his hand.

"The red door, mister? I will show you."

He lost his wallet in the hutong without knowing it. Then he saw the door. Red like Kimberly's kiss on the grassy banks of a forgotten night. Red like the scarlet leaves of a forest he once knew. He realized Greshen was the only real companion in his life, rote as their meetings were. This fact alone invoked a yearning to see her.

"Did you have yourself a fine woman there?" Greshen asked his first night back in Vegas. "I hear Asian women suck good cock."

They were in their usual penthouse in the Bengal. Outside the oversized windows the lights of Vegas were dancing, somersaulting, in ways that the lights of Beijing never would. He'd already come inside her, inside a thinly ribbed condom that was like an extra titillating layer of vulva.

"Does it bother you that I sleep with other women?"

Immediately he was irritated with himself for asking the question. But he felt something inside him give, a minute door in some shadowed corner of his experience. Blood percolated to his temples.

"Seriously, does it bother you? Especially since you fuck other men for money?"

Her fabricated face, the blonde trimmings, fell forward as though uncoupled from their mounting. Then the eyes lifted slowly. Her nose quivered in a pre-sneeze, but no sound followed. He watched a single tear squeeze itself free from the greenish clamp of her right eye.

"I'm not ashamed of what I am," she said.

The head remounted on the neck, as if hoisted by wires. A look of haughtiness returned, confident as precision steel.

"But you will be someday, Stamer, and your partner running around with mob goons. All the money will dry up, and you'll be ashamed of yourself. You won't be able to buy anything like me."

He slapped her hard. She fell whimpering onto the unmade bed. He'd never before touched her face, and its texture registered between his palm and brain. He wasn't surprised that he'd hit her but was surprised her face felt so real and soft and human. He wanted to feel it again. He almost apologized, almost reached out and touched her tear-wet cheek.

"Get out," he said.

He turned his back as she collected her things and left his life forever.

• • •

LI STANDS ON THE small promontory taking pictures. Droplets bead the rim of his lens, but he's unconcerned. His fingers riffle the wetness as he focuses forward, snapping the shutter closed and open and closed and open in a delicate-sounding movement akin to butterfly wings. He wants to catch the essence of the mist. He wants to catch the essence of a light wave, to know it as sharply as a kiss—to freeze it, isolate it, reveal it not merely as a trick of physics but as something concrete, a singular pain, like his pain, his selfishness, as carved and resplendent as a glass tear.

When he turns back to the trail, Stamer Stone and Dorle Wasser appear like tandem ghosts on the mountainside. The closer he gets, slinging his camera back on his shoulder, the more he perceives their weight, his own weight. They're all carrying something up the mountainside that makes them real.

• • •

MORE THAN HALFWAY THROUGH an ignoble decade, the first decade of the new millennium, Stamer couldn't ignore evidence that the firm he and Forster had created was in mortal danger. Property values in southern Nevada had ballooned, and AmerzWest Capital Corp. had honed in on certain profitable ventures just outside the city proper. Because every builder in the country had wanted a piece of the boom—like a new wave of prospectors armed with bulldozers instead of pickaxes—

Forster had devised a mechanism to facilitate their wishes. He'd drafted a prospectus and solicited investors from across the globe. He'd pooled their money and begun offering short-term, high-interest loans to qualified developers and contractors. The firm's contracts with investors were promissory notes that set a repayment schedule and high returns. The firm's construction loans were to be secured with real estate collateral; the deeds would transfer to AmerzWest Capital Corp. if loan recipients defaulted. This two-way revolving loan pool, which Forster had nicknamed "tiger's blood," became a ferocious engine of suburban growth.

The county's planning offices, miles away from Custer Square, were inundated with new subdivision requests. Staff approvals came quick and steady, along with variances, tweaks in code, revised design standards—everything and anything to keep the engine running, to keep collecting what had become the greatest amount of filing fees, hookup fees, and ancillary taxes in county history. The heads of the planning department even gave themselves and senior staff members modest pay raises—beyond normal step increases and cost-of-living adjustments—as a reward for successfully managing the heavy increase in workload.

Standing in his office in the Bengal Tower, Stamer would use binoculars to view the new development on the edge of the city: the scraped and graded lots, the half-built homes gleaming with the raw ocher of plywood, the lone fire hydrants standing at the unbuilt edges of the new neighborhoods, where the lacquered black roads emptied into the shimmering desert. In this way, the city seemed to be spreading incrementally, converting the sand and weeds into its own likeness.

For the first few years, profits were strong. Investors saw returns of 12-15 percent, which Forster used to attract even more capital, to pay even higher returns. But one afternoon Stamer received a call from the city recorder's office. It was not the recorder herself, but a secretary in the office who informed him that AmerzWest Capital Corp. was not listed as a trustee on the latest round of parceling. She told him she was an investor in the company herself and had found it strange. Stamer assured her it was most likely a glitch. After hanging up, he took the elevator up to Forster's office on the twenty-sixth floor.

"He's in a meeting with Karl," said his friend's secretary, a statuary blonde who could have passed for Greshen's twin.

"It's okay. Let me through."

Forster's office was decorated with artifacts from his Salt Lake City abode: the painting of the woman, the tiger, which he'd first seen all those years ago, vivid then, vivid now, and the wooden masks with carved fangs. But there were new items as well: jade statuettes from China, rain sticks from Africa, a rare flute from Norway. His friend's eclecticism was splayed in well-lit wall-niches and narrow glass cases sided with espresso-stained wood. The high chamber of the suite was furnished with tables of the same wood and maroon leather chairs. A sofa stretched along the far wall of glass paneling, which was structured so clear and seamlessly that standing there, one would lose himself in the city lights as if in a swarm of stars, immersed in the bright palpitations of new galaxies, new planets.

Both Forster and Karl were bent over the coffee table in front of the sofa, snorting lines of cocaine.

"I heard from the recorder's office just now we don't have a line on the new properties," Stamer said, fiercely, standing directly behind them.

The sight of Karl infuriated him. And it was Karl who first looked up, his combed grayish hair disheveled in greasy wisps, his retro glasses, their heavy square frame, somehow insulting, imposing.

"No one's got clear title anymore," Karl said, sniffing the drug from his upper lip.

"What the hell do you mean?"

Forster put his nose to the table and snorted with a sensuous rip. Then his head shot up.

"Everything is papered over, my friend. The guys we're loaning to no longer have sole interest. Everyone's in the bubble. Do you understand? It's impossible to get a line because no one knows where the line ends."

Stamer noticed fresh lines around his friend's eyes, finely etched like score marks. His skin was discolored, alternating between blotchy white and purplish pink.

"We're telling investors these are secure loans," Stamer said. "We're lying."

Karl squeaked with laughter. He threw his head back into the couch like it were a bowling ball tossed aside by his surging high. The room tilted. City lights throbbed and twinkled.

"We're telling them what they need to hear so we can make them rich," Forster answered. "It is what they want to hear. This is the covenant, remember? As long as they're getting paid, they don't care whose name is on a deed in some dusty office."

"What if it buckles?"

Karl spoke with his eyes closed, head wheeling: "Everything will be taken care of. I guarantee it."

When Stamer looked back to Forster, his friend showed a wild, wavering smile breaking his face into even finer wrinkles. Like a man ecstatic in a lightning storm. Then the smile flattened, and seriousness weighed down his lips.

"I need you to do something, friend."

Stamer was silent. He was thinking about Greshen—a sudden impulse to call her before remembering it was impossible now. She had disappeared from the Bengal Tower.

"Okay."

"I need you to go up to northeastern Nevada with the water authority. They're making a trip up there next week. We're running out of water rights, Stamer. We can't build more houses unless we have water. You've heard about the pipeline. You know we need it. They know we need it. Your job is to make sure we get it."

• • •

Stamer massages his forehead with his fingertips, the falls whelming his mind's tunnels.

"I'm thinking of heading back down alone," Dorle says. "Maybe enough exercise for today?"

Her show of sovereignty instantly hollows him. She stands a vertical foot above him. The damp blue cotton around her stomach trembles with her breathing. He feels the urge to throw himself against the soft wall of her body, to bury himself in the damp mounds of her breasts. Her neck glistens and drips with the mist, her own sweat, the water running through everything. Why the need to grab her? Why the need to own her? What is he scared of?

"Come on," he says. "Don't chicken out. It's a short climb to the top."

• • •

The last summer he worked for AmerzWest Capital Corp., Stamer drove to Eastern Nevada in a rented Buick sedan with two black briefcases in the back. The assistant director of the water authority cautioned against traveling together. The authority had already made market-rate offers to those ranchers holding vast underground water rights in Skull Springs Valley. Stamer's briefcases were to sweeten the deal for two families who'd held out. There was a million in cash for each, off the books, if they agreed to sell to the authority within a week. Because the ranchers didn't know he was coming, and because environmentalists had formed a picket line around the authority's satellite office in Ely, Stamer had to proceed with stealth and discretion. He had the private numbers of both ranchers and planned to set up private meetings. Where and how were yet to be determined.

In all his time in Las Vegas, Stamer had never traveled to the rural parts of the state. Now he found tortured mountain ranges rising from the sage-dotted crust of the desert, like shoulder blades rotating sharply from the hard-brown, knuckled back of the earth. Within their sinewy hardness, amid their grave, petrified faces, he descried peculiar softness. A furry sash of pine trees on a bare shoulder. A bank of aspen in a barren fold. These soft things were tender to the eye, secret flourishes in the dry and monstrous silence. They reminded him of all those years back when he had first crossed the Rocky Mountains.

Ely was a stark town on the edge of the mountains. Stamer found a cheap hotel room and unloaded his luggage. He stashed the two briefcases under the bed, shaved, showered, dressed in jeans, short-sleeved plaid, hiking boots, then headed downtown in the cool sharp air of the high mountain desert.

The Deuce Heart Bar was on the bottom floor of an old stick-built hotel, painted in chintz-white and pasty-blue. Cigarette smoke clouded the air. The old-timey wooden bar sat in dark yellow light cast from a line of painted bulbs above the back mirror. Stamer felt faces turn and eyes poke as he sat down and asked for a Bud Light. The barkeep was a scrawny man with watery eyes and a beard like thistledown in a breeze. He wore a gnawed, greasy, gray felt cowboy hat.

"Two even," he said.

Stamer paid and sipped the beer from the cold mouth of the bottle. His teeth clinked against the glass lips. On the other side of the bar two aged cowboys in stained denim and straw hats were talking to each other low and serious. Stamer somehow intuited they were the ranchers he wanted, and as he strained to listen to their conversation, he felt the world spin around and around, as if all his knowledge—all he'd learned and practiced and habituated in his own precise character—was suddenly naught, stretched thin and pinned to the edge of an immense, unraveling secret. The air buzzed faintly. His skin was hot and itchy.

"If we do this, we make out like bandits," one of the men said. "We never work another damn day in our lives."

"How much?" the other man asked.

The language hummed in Stamer's ears. No one else could hear it. The barkeep's back was turned as he sorted lemon wedges in a plastic container. Billiard balls cracked in a hazy corner.

The first man nodded with a circumspect grin.

"A mil each."

The world spun and spun and spun. Stamer guzzled the beer, which helped stabilize the sticky wooden floor, then asked for another and began nursing it more slowly.

"Well, hell, I wouldn't even know what to do with that kind of money," the second man said. "I wouldn't know what to do with myself. I love working the place. This is my home. I know everything about it. I ain't got one idea what to do otherwise...

"Plus," the man continued more warmly, as if recovering from the cold hard shock of the cash, "those sons of bitches will draw the aquifers down to nothing. They say they won't, but I know for a fact they will. They'll suck the grass from under our feet, and we won't have a damn thing left."

Stamer paid for his second beer and fled the Deuce Heart Bar. Outside, the air was an astringent on the wound of his mind. He didn't know what bothered him more: that Forster had obviously contacted the men and not trusted him enough to follow through, or that the men were forming their own ideas about money and value and the future of a remote corner of the world he had no interest in. Buzzed from the beers, he walked back to the hotel noticing how quiet and bleak the town's buildings appeared in the queer amalgam of streetlight and moonlight.

His hotel door was cracked open. The lights were off. A human smell, an oily smell tinged with the scent of wild mint, issued from the room. Fuck, he thought. Maybe Forster and Karl had set him up. He thought about running to the car and taking off into the night. But something about the smell was familiar. He swung the door open and entered the room. A man sat on the edge of the bed, his silhouette like a torn piece of cloth.

"You still got the knife I gave you?"

The voice was deep and rough. Stamer was speechless. In his head he saw a city beneath the mountains, a wild and overgrown woodland, a campfire flickering in the purple dark.

"Red Cloud?"

"You must leave this place."

Stamer's hand groped the wall for the light switch.

"No, don't," said Red Cloud.

"Buh...but..." Stamer stammered for the first time in decades. "How did you know I was here?"

"I have seen a man fall from a tower in the sky. When he hits the ground, people are dead. The grass is weeping. The grass is screaming. People are dead. I don't know how you know this man who falls from the sky, but you must leave here and never come back."

Red Cloud rose and lumbered toward the door. Stamer moved aside to let him pass. He watched the figure descend the metal stairs of the motel and walk toward the highway. He neared a streetlamp, and just when Stamer thought he'd see his old friend's face in the raining light, Red Cloud vanished.

Stamer woke with his smartphone in his hand. It was the first of its kind, the screen as sleek and seamless as a blade—an opaqueness, a blindness, the violence of kings encased in glass, a screaming tomb. He thought about calling Forster but decided there was no point. He rose and washed himself in the motel sink, splashing warm water on his face. When he looked into the mirror, the whites of his eyes were coagulated red. The stubble on his chin was bristling whitish gray. He realized he was an old man.

He checked out of the motel and followed the yawning highway across the mountain-crests and valley-troughs of the Great Basin. In Austin, he threw his phone in a dumpster behind a quaint diner. He kept driving. He slept overnight in his car parked off a random dirt road. In Carson City, he returned the rental car to a chain outlet, and with cash from one of the briefcases bought an old gray Ford truck from a Lithuanian car dealer. The truck looked like his first truck. It ran rickety but worked. He stopped at an army surplus store and loaded up on supplies. Then he drove south along the eastern boundary of the Sierra Nevada. At some point, he crossed over. The mountains were more beautiful than anything else in his life. The granite peaks glowed pink in the sunset like stone bouquets. The light suffused the manifold surfaces of stone but also limned something within, as if the inanimate, implacable world had a heart, too, which, like his heart, thrummed with energy. He had a strong intuition that the light came from both within and without. He knew where he wanted to go. And he knew that once there, he would never leave.

● ● ●

HE WANTS ME, DORLE thinks, seeing the way Stamer's gaze has softened, unsure of itself. He stands on the trail below her, like a dumbfounded, wistful plant reaching for the sun. The heart is such a senseless thing, she thinks. Pumping nonsense through the body. His kiss was like sugar in my blood, she thinks. Melting, gone.

She imagines her daughter, what she'd have to do to make things right. There's enough space now between herself and the past. It's like she's looking down on the scene of the accident. Christmas Eve. 2005. Blood gleaming in the white beard of Chester Winfield. An old, gregarious Farewellian who'd dressed up as Santa Claus. He lay dead in the street. A huge ragged pine lay atop her sedan. She was drunk and had chopped it down from the courthouse lawn. Because Jason and Dora wouldn't go into the mountains with her. The tree was lashed to the car with bungee cords and duct tape.

"It wasn't my fault," she tells the judge. "He was jaywalking at night."

"He was going to see his grandchildren," answers the red, splenetic face. "Do you understand that, Ms. Wasser? He was going to see his grandchildren."

A Santa hat lying on the asphalt, bent like an empty, kicked-in stocking. The yellow-haired reporter—Jules, Julia?—scribbling in her notebook. Then the headline announcing it to the world:

'It Wasn't My Fault!' Daughter of Wasser Vineyard Sentenced to Six Years for Vehicular Manslaughter.

Jesus, it was my fault, she thinks. She laughs. A scoffing laugh. A tragic contralto. She sees the aberration of her life like a smoldering wreck at the feet of the cliffs. Puny screams against the stone.

"What's up?" Stamer asks.

She remembers the shower. Dora licks the water on her lips.

"It was my fault," she tells Stamer.

"What was?"

"Killing a man. Losing my daughter," she says, but he can't hear her.

• • •

IN THE YEARS AND months before the accident, when Dorle was no longer working at the restaurant, Dora grew into daddy's little girl. Although she was Dorle in miniature—the same dirty blond hair and blue eyes, the same small, defiant mouth, the same thin, stem-like body—she had her father's calm, dutiful demeanor. Dorle didn't know if this demeanor was learned or inherited, but she flinched every time her daughter stopped her mid-sentence, shook her child head, then fixed her lambent eyes upon her with that stern kind of patience that renders judgment and necessitates correction. It was the kind of patience Jason practiced and exhibited daily. The harder Dorle tried, no matter the pursuit, the more Dora resisted. *No, mom, we can't do that. It's silly. It won't work.*

For Dora's tenth birthday, Dorle traveled to the city and found the best jeweler on Market Street and bought her daughter a pair of pearl earrings. That night in the apartment, the family enjoyed Dora's

favorite dinner of spaghetti and meatballs, followed by German chocolate cake, racked with ten flaming candles, and orange sherbet.

"Make a wish, honey," Jason urged.

Dora sighed, as though tasked with a chore.

"I wish daddy would let me work in the restaurant."

Her breath blew spastic across the cake. The candles flickered
then fell quiet with smoke. Dorle's heart sank.

"That's very sweet," Jason said, his voice wet-sounding, happy.

"Here," Dorle interrupted.

She thrust the tiny gift-wrapped box onto the table.

"A special present for my baby."

Dora looked skeptical, yet gingerly unfastened the bow, unfolded
the paper. When she removed the lid, her eyes flickered like the candles.
Dorle saw it. Her eyes flickered, and her small, defiant mouth opened
in a half-smile.

"They're pearls," Dorle explained, "the finest saltwater pearls I
could find."

Dora pulled her eyes from the gift and looked at her father, whose
face had tilted with concern, mouth pouted in a frown. He drew a
thoughtful breath, deepening his concern, and Dorle could see, in less
than a second, her daughter's joy collapse and disappear altogether.

"I don't think we can afford them, mom."

Dora put the lid back on the box. Like her husband, Dorle also
breathed ponderously. The sadness inside her drowned any fight she
had left. In confirmation of her daughter's wishes, she nodded.

"I want a new house," she told Jason that night in bed, after
downing a bottle of birthday wine she'd picked up with the cake.

His left eyebrow arched but was quickly reined in by his cool,
tense eyes.

"How long you been drinking again?"

His concern was likewise cool and perfunctory. His voice—so
flat, so rote, so weary—enraged her. She hated his voice.

"What kind of man raises a family in an apartment?"

Her words bit into the serene planes of his face until, she thought, she detected a twitch of anger.

"I mean, honestly, for crying out loud, how long are we going to live in this dump?"

His face grew more agitated. His hazel eyes began blinking in tiny spasms.

"This dump was good enough for you when we got married. Besides Dora, what's changed? We got two bedrooms. We're not having another kid."

"You decided that, not me!" her voice smashed against the bedroom walls.

Jason mashed his lips together in his best verisimilitude of anger. A defiant breath chuffed from his nose. Like the snort of a horse spurred.

"No, Dorle, you decided that, not me. You decided that when you couldn't stop drinking."

The rising edge in his voice cut through her. She'd never seen his face so animated, almost incandescent with ire.

"Well—"

She wavered against the heat and the pain of his assertion.

"You know it's true, too," he persisted. "You're a screwup."

The word "screw" hissed like a sliver of ice in her brain.

"Maybe," she said. "But you're a lousy lay."

Smack. His hand fell across her face so fast and unexpectedly she thought she was blacking out from the wine. Everything flashed and flickered, and her eyes were stinging, and she was crying. Then Jason was back in his dull monotone voice, repeating over and over how sorry he was. She turned on her side and sniveled into the night. His hand landed on her hip, tentatively, and trembled against her body. He told her a new house wasn't such a bad idea.

What they could afford was a two-bedroom brick bungalow, built in the 1920s, that sat about the same distance from the diner as their current apartment. It was a craftsman-style bungalow, with two brick pillars supporting a handsome front porch and a gable peeking out from the attic. Upon seeing the exterior, Dorle immediately thought of opulent flowerpots and elegant wrought iron fencing. The interior, however, depressed her just as quickly. The carpet in the living room was filthy and reeked of cigarette smoke; she knew they couldn't afford to replace it. The appliances and cabinets in the kitchen were older than those in the apartment. The bedrooms were narrow, the closets were cramped, and even the one bathroom was a letdown—bigger than they were used to, yet, with its small white tile and mildewed corners, clinical, irremediable.

But it was a house. There was a backyard, and a fireplace, and a large, empty basement that smelled of mold. When Dorle walked down the creaking stairs, beneath age-dark floor joists cobwebbed like a crypt, she shuddered. A bare bulb hung in the dark, lighting the way back to her father's cellar, the husk of his body, the vintages sleeping in their stone niches.

"I don't like it," she told Jason. "It's too old and creepy."

He answered with exasperation.

"It's the only house for sale in Farewell we can afford. It's either this, or we stay in the apartment."

Not long after the move, Dora figured out that her mother disliked the basement; for she insisted that dry foods be kept in the kitchen, and she'd only venture downstairs to do laundry, staying no longer than five minutes at a time.

"Dad says he's gonna make the basement a game room," Dora relayed one afternoon, watching her mother's face shift in aversion.

"The basement?" she asked.

The obvious fear in her mother's voice stirred Dora in a strange way. It was like the tiny, terrible thrill she experienced when digging her fingers into the soft spots of a pear, pushing the bruises until the skin split and sloughed off.

"Dad wants to put a TV down there. And some chairs. He also said a ping-pong table if it can fit."

Dorle's face was scrunched now, straining in disbelief. Her wariness, her degradation, coursed as fresh, triumphant power through Dora's young, pubescent body. Not unlike the exhilaration the girl felt when touching herself.

"That's a silly idea," Dorle protested, her voice shrill with a note of hysteria. "You have a beautiful room to yourself, and we already have a TV in the living room."

Not unlike the warm, pervading satiation the girl felt devouring one of her father's hamburgers at the diner.

"Well, that's what dad said," Dora argued.

That's what dad said.

That's what dad said.

Dorle was tearing toward the kitchen. She found the vodka in the cupboard, hidden behind the taller bottles of cooking oil and the cylindrical forest of spices. As she dug into the crowded space, a plastic container rolled out and thunked on the floor.

"What are you doing, mom?" the girl's voice rose from behind.

Dorle stopped herself, belly smashed against the counter, arm crammed in the cabinet. She was almost panting.

"Nothing, Dora. Nothing that concerns you."

She had her hand on the bottle. She could feel the cool slender neck of it.

"Mom?"

Silence.

"Mom?"

The word hung in the air like a malediction. Dorle pulled out the bottle, knocking more spices onto the floor, and turned around to face her daughter.

"Yes, Dora, what can I do for you?"

The girl standing before her was no longer a child. No longer her child. Not the babe she'd once coddled and un-coddled, whom she'd once held in the shower as a shining testament to all she felt as good.

The girl was now a woman with beautiful mocking eyes and a dissatis-
fied frown. Dorle saw the face of her own mother.

"You little bitch!" she snarled. "How dare you judge me!"

Dora's eyes flashed with fear.

"Mom, dad said—"

"Shut up! Just shut up!"

Dorle raised the bottle of vodka over her head. The liquid looked
as smooth and transparent as the inside of an ice floe.

"See this? Your mother likes to drink. So what? Go run and tell
your daddy!"

She unscrewed the cap and took a burning gulp. She coughed
against the fumes. When she recovered her breath and looked up, Dora
was crying. Dora the child. Dora her baby. Just as guilt pierced her
heart, the alcohol hit her bloodstream, washed her thoughts warm.
Then she could hear Dora and Jason talking in the distance, murmuring. She stumbled to the sofa in the living room. She lay down and fell
asleep before they could say anything else against her.

From that point on, Dorle's unhappiness swelled deeper than
the oceans. She drank every day until the flood of alcohol turned
the world inside out, until the bottom of every hole she feared overwhelmed what was left of her senses—darkness palpable, hideous, roiling in the bottom of her thoughts, spiraling around the root of her life,
her mistakes. She'd turn away and drift in a fugue state. The faces of
people she knew became strange fish, blobs of watery color, their voices
distorted by fathoms of alcohol, their words wavy and sickening.

Occasionally, nearing the surface of lucidity, she would remember
things. The red stag hidden in the alder brakes behind the white house.
A fir tree pointed like a steeple, gilded by sunlight. A pearl earring glistening in her mother's ear. All phantoms now. She tried to grab them,
these memories, to pull herself to clarity. She reached out but found
nothing to grasp, only the evanescence of these things, like segments
of a rainbow dissolving in darkness. She drank more, cursed more. She

swirled back down in drowsiness and bitterness, back to the bottom where there was at least a vague pain she could hold onto.

There was a day in November, weeks before the accident, closer to the surface of reality, when she realized her daughter had begun a new life with her father at the restaurant. Dora had become a busser, learning the ropes of her father's business and splitting tips with the waiters. But what had started as a part-time weekend shift became her full-time absence from the house. The basement was vacant. Its new furnishings—giant beanbag chairs, television and VCR, a cheap and rickety cabinet that stored movies—sat unused, collecting a special kind of dust Dorle detested. It was warm dust, sticky dust, dust alive with decay—dirt, dander, pollen, mold, mildew all bound together in an iridescent film that squeaked over the furniture and spread through her mind with a vile shimmer.

"Why the fuck did we buy a house if you're never gonna be there?"

The question screeched through the restaurant ambiance like the boiling whistle of a teakettle. Dora's face reddened with embarrassment. She fled to the kitchen to find her father. The patrons sitting in the booths stared at the woman with shocked eyes and open mouths.

"Dorle," sounded Jason's voice from the service window, the same window from which she'd once taken his incomparable gift of a hamburger. "This isn't the place to do this, Dorle."

His voice was steady and reassuring. There was something of her father's voice in it. It soothed and softened her anger.

"We have a full house here today, as you can see. You're drunk. We'd like you to leave."

The double doors clattered as Dora returned. She was shaking her head vigorously, sobbing, as though trying to ward off the cruel fact of the moment. What was left of the mother's rage, the wave of indignation that had carried her to the restaurant, broke in futility. She collapsed to the floor.

• • •

"CAN'T WE LEAVE THE past behind?" Stamer says. "Won't you come to the top with me?"

Dorle shakes her head. She realizes a man like Stamer will never fill her up. Just like her, he's been taught to take, not to give.

No, she can't live in that world anymore. She won't be going to the top with him. These holes, she thinks, these cellars, she thinks, passed from generation to generation. Inheritances of shadow. And everyone desperate to backfill.

Dora needs her mother, she thinks. The touch of love, she thinks. She laughs. She wonders at the simplicity of it. The mystery of the self, the way we hack it to pieces, and from the pieces build shrines, stilted, ridiculous, then tear them down to start over, frenzied in our incompletion, learning only in the slack, the letting go, does light find its quiet and ineffable fulfillment.

Yes, it's simple, she thinks. She will start over with her daughter, one visit at a time. And she will try to make things right with the family of the man she killed. Her head tingles with the hope of reconciliation. Tears sting her cheeks in slick, salty streaks, a piquant burn. Yet she breathes easy, rippling inly, in love with the soft space of the moment, the firm, moist ground, the basement smell of the earth, her feet and legs and lower back pleasantly sore and radiating warm, satisfying pain.

"I'm not going to the top, Stamer, but maybe I'll see you and Li back down in the valley."

Her words feel like redemption, like time made whole. She looks past Stamer's befuddled face and sees Li off-trail, leaning into a shaded bank. She sees the color purple there. From a sliver of soil, between moss-bearded boulders, floppy purple flowers nod from small, slender ladders of green leaves.

Li grazes the clusters with his hand. He plucks off a head and raises it to his face. Up close, the corolla appears more blue than purple, its inner throat a streak of deep, bright yellow. Greedily he tears off the stamens. He digs his finger into the middle of the blossom and hits the ripe ovary. With his fingernail, he lifts the weary style. It's thin and limp like a human hair. When he removes his finger, it nods back over, as if guided by some instinct of self-protection. It's pathetic. He's pathetic. A suffocated cry writhes within. He kisses his fingertips and carries the kiss to the tip of the style, the stigma. It feels like cool, shredded flesh. He gasps, admitting what he already knows to be true. *Danyu, my yinghua.*

●　●　●

HE WAS GAGGED, BLINDFOLDED, but not beaten. There was little driving. Then hands on either arm. There was a hurried and clunky descent of stairs. Then the smell of sewer. Wet grime. Rusted infrastructure. For a minute, he thought they'd taken him to Xanadu. But no other voices materialized. He hoped no other comrades had been exposed. They shackled him and left him alone in the dark, his mind reeling with images. Danyu's delicate lips. The red door of his now-famous painting. Zhou's cockeyed face burning with desire, hardening with bitterness. Then his father—an image of his father struck him with unusual force, a punch of light, and he realized the blindfold had been removed.

The real man stood before him. His small, indestructible eyes bore through the dim space. The eyes stay fastened on Li as the man lowered himself into a chair on the other side of a plain wooden table. They didn't speak. Luduan's stare grew harder, and the immobility of the face, its cold and sterile oppression, angered Li. He stared back as hard as he could, but the expressionless eyes didn't budge.

Father and son remained in this silent and frozen state for at least an hour. At times, Li started sniffling, not from sadness, but from thirst, growing hunger, allergies. He allowed himself to blink, at first quickly, then indulgently, soothing his sore eyes. Every time he did this, he imagined his father was also blinking, taking advantage of the moment. Once, suddenly cracking his eyes open as if to catch Luduan in the act, he was disappointed to find the man's face hadn't changed the slightest. Eventually, Luduan removed something from his shirt pocket. He dropped it onto the table, making a tinkle in the silence. It was a paper clip. Nothing more.

"You will tell me who is running the operation."

The words cut low and sharp. Li hadn't even seen his father's lips move. There was something entirely irrational in the stern assurance of the face, in the infallibility of the words. Irrational and unaccountable and terrific. Li felt a tingle of fear at the back of his throat.

"Father, why am I here?" he asked, his own voice sounding rattled and compromised.

Luduan's hand flared up like a flag, demanding immediate cessation of questions, fortifying the implacable eyes.

"What is it you think I've done?"

BOOM! The flag-hand was now a fist pounded on the table—a single deafening blow, then silence.

"You will tell me who is running the operation."

The tingling fear in Li's throat extended into a keening blade. He swallowed against the fear, feeling the dry, heavy wrack of his Adam's apple.

"Does my mother know I'm here?"

Luduan's head finally moved, but only in the tremor of an impatient sigh. He picked up the paper clip and began unfolding it carefully. At the same time another man entered the room, a young, plain-clothes agent not much older than Li. He had no expression on his face other than some habituated sternness of duty. He unshackled Li's arm from the back of the chair. Before Li could make a fist, or recoil in any way, the young agent had Li's wrist in an iron grip and was flattening Li's hand onto the table. The surface was cool against his palm. He looked up at his father. He thought he saw a flash of doubt, a flicker of shame. But Luduan rose quietly to his feet and approached his son without a word—

Li feels the mountainside behind the purple flowers. A concave slab of granite, slate-gray, smelling of stone-must.

"I'm going to head down," Dorle tells him.

He ignores her, ignores Stamer, and returns to the sunny lookout over the falls. He now observes the lone pine jutting up between the boulders. He doesn't know it's the gnarled relic of a bristlecone pine. He just sees its jagged reddish stump. Like a broken totem on the edge of the precipice. Behind it the veil of mist fluxes and shines in the sunlight. He doesn't know that the tree has lived above the river for thousands of years, before the birth of Christ, and that despite its countenance, its wood is still alive; its roots live in the secret moist spaces between the stone. He doesn't know that every spring a handful of saplings shoot up between the rocks and reach for sunlight only to discover the duplicity of existence, the terrible scarcity of resources beneath them, the preclusion of their growth, the withering of their life. He doesn't know that the bird now landing on the tree's knotted bough is a western tanager. It has a bright yellow breast, like the inside of the flower he destroyed, and a scarlet head, like a living flame, a stroke of fire. Its color defies the air. It defies him as he defied her.

He turns back to the trail, and he feels his neon sneakers gripping the slippery earth, sliding, sliding—

The metal paper clip sliding under his fingernail.

Luduan's impassive face. A mechanical problem, yes, to break his son.

The metal paper clip probing under his fingernail, tickling the tip of rarified flesh.

Then Luduan's quick, efficient grunt and a sudden stabbing motion.

Fuck! God of mercy! Li is screaming his head off—the most exquisite pain—he's screaming his head off as the paper clip pierces and pops the heart of a secret nerve.

Luduan grunts, he grunts like a real beast, like a man finding himself in animal disrepute, chewing through it, confident in the transgression, the retribution against rules that would keep him forever debased. He's grunting, extracting shrill, quavering cries from his only son, feeding on the humiliation. That of his country, its history, his family, his son.

Li tries to move his hand but can't. His blood is coloring the plain table in brilliant splats and smears. He thinks of the red door he can never uncreate, and then of Danyu's lips, like the carved, puckered flesh of a cherry tree.

"My *yinghua*!" he cries. "Zhh—"

He almost says the name of his teacher but can't.

The young, dull attendant tightens his grip, nonchalantly.

Luduan grows quiet. He returns to the other side of the table.

"You will tell me who is running the operation," he says.

No, no. Li hears his own voice jagged within him, broken by pain, but still alive, summoning strength. He pushes the voice up until, hoarse and hot, it breaks from his mouth:

"You're a coward," he utters. "I'm ashamed to be your son."

At these words, Luduan's face finally gives. The eyes and mouth, so long composed, are torn apart by rage. He jumps up, knocking his chair over, and charges his son while drawing a pistol from his side.

Li sees the black barrel coming like a pugnacious snout. It's coming to rout his worst terror—not of death, but of incompletion, of work unfinished, uncertain status, the confusion of love and hate still raging like a waterfall all around him. He thinks he will die when the barrel is suddenly whipped around and, without a shot, the pistol butt comes down instead, smacking his head into dreamlessness—

He's pacing back and forth between the jumbled overlook, the single pine, now birdless, and the purple flowers growing in the mountain. The lies, the things he's told himself, wriggle inside, struggle to stay alive. They twist and twitch against the truth. Dorle, half-turned, studies him curiously. Her face is bright with the pride of her own exertion and renewal, and Li, conscious of her newfound dignity, flinches. He used to know what to do, feeling so locked and hard and leaden. He used to know how to break through, open doors, fire the air.

But there are no more doors. Everything's burned for good. Deep dark red. Ash-gray. His head is throbbing as if gripped by a steel band.

Wait, he thinks. What if I could just—

What?

Paint. Feel that new life. The surge, the burn.

It's gone. Dead.

What if I could just—

What?

What?

I don't know. How can it return? How can I feel things again after losing them?

He looks back at Dorle, her fresh air of resilience.

She's got it, he thinks. I should paint her, catch her in the act. But she's turning away from us. She doesn't want our fear and desperation. She doesn't want our devastation.

It's too late to start over. It's too late.

What if I could just—

What?

What?

Remember? You thought painting was everything. You thought you could make restitution with the currency of your genius.

Fool!

You thought you could build a virtuous world through your art, as if art were the sum of all virtue.

But you never cared about virtue, did you?

Li is roiling now, in a vast, voiding anguish. He wonders if any of it were real, his life, his art, the things he once felt so strongly, like bright fire fading into stolid hues.

Danyu. Danyu was real—

"What do you give up by loving me?"

Zhou asked the question mere days after Li was tortured by his own father, as if it were the only pertinent question in the face of collapse and dissolution.

Zhou then reached down and squeezed his student's cock through his pants. Li groaned in unexpected pleasure.

"Stop it! Stop it!"

Zhou squeezed harder and worked his hand over the clothed erection. Li saw his teacher's eye, the maimed eye, hanging sickly, trembling, from the hook of a sardonic grin.

"What are you afraid of?" Zhou pressed. "What are these loyalties?"

"Enough!" Li screamed. "My heart does not belong to you! Accept it, Zhou"—

Danyu was real. Danyu was a real person. He couldn't describe her if he tried. He couldn't paint her if he tried. Maybe he never tried because deep down in the charnel house of his vanity he knew she was too real, too alive, too complex a being to be reduced to lines in his enraged and grandiose sketches—

"It was Danyu, you fool!" Zhou told him viciously, gleefully.

Li blinked with incipient betrayal. The world was whooshing apart, losing its definition. "How do you know?"

"You think your father didn't get to her first?"

"She wouldn't speak against me."

"What if she spoke against me and that led to you? How can you be so blind?"—

He turns back to the granite slab. He braces his arm on the wall and presses his head into the crook of his elbow. He begins to sob. Then he hears people on the path behind him, and he stops, holds himself still.

"What's wrong?" Dorle asks.

Her hand touches his shoulder. It feels warm and vital, like a message from another world.

But how can he tell her that it was all a lie, the art, the movement, the revolution? That it was little more than a secret boys club, inane, vainglorious, enamored only with the romance of war and rebellion? How can he tell her that he failed to protect what mattered most?

He knows, with biting clarity, that he's failed as an artist. He's failed as an artist because he's failed as a human being.

His sobs break anew, staccato against the stone—

"I know a man who can do it quick," Zhou says.

The teacher's overwrought face. A grotesque cynicism.

"How?" Li asks.

"That's not important. What's important is we protect Xanadu."

"You mean we protect ourselves"—

"Liar!" Li bellows into the canyon.

Falling water.

Streaks of platinum-red.

Shrieks as the knife slips between her shoulder blades.

He hits the stone, smacks it, kicks it.

Dorle is backing away, apologizing to fellow hikers gathered around the scene.

Stamer is shaking his head, looking terrified, as though surrounded by ghastly nymphs and sprites, by the ghosts of all the people he almost loved.

Then Li is turning around, wiping his face with his arm. He grunts like a bear and charges the sunny overlook and its lone broken tree.

Dorle reaches for him, sees blood gleaming in the beard of Chester Winfield. She screams.

I love you, Dora. Please forgive me. God help us.

She grabs the tail of his shirt, skidding, stumbling knee-first onto the ground. The shirt rips in her hand then slips out, propelling Li's body forward with new force. He's hurtling toward the edge, the clean break of sunlight. She's on her feet again lunging after him. She reaches out one last time just as he throws himself over the cliff. She barely touches the torn fray of his shirt—like the soft yet rough texture of a child's rag doll—then she's weightless in the air, the dark shape of Li sailing beneath her.

● ● ●

THE INDIAN GRANDMOTHER SEES it first: two figures flailing in the air beside the falls. Down they go in silence. And she thinks she's seen two ghosts. Or two demons. Quick as a blink of an eye. She looks to her daughter and granddaughter also standing on the bridge over the river. Their faces betray nothing except impatience with the day, with her, the elder, and her slow, deliberate, sacred parceling of life.

The way she takes each step with an expression of mistrust, as though doubting the ground on which she walks, and then marking whatever distance she has gained with low, humming mantras.

The way she stares at everything, especially other people, with hard, knowing eyes, as though keeping constant vigil on the world and the facts around her, protective of whatever knowledge she has earned.

But they don't know her, these women, her own kin. They don't know that given the right conditions, the right opportunity, her compassion would open like a flower and her emotions rejoice with whatever song the world had left. They don't know how bad she wants to cry for all the things she can't give them.

No, she thinks, they didn't see the two dark shapes slipping from the cliffs, staining the air for a second. Like moths of ink she used to see in her nightmares. Now an inky chill in her thoughts. And she thinks the bridge will be the end of her hike today.

● ● ●

THE WOMAN IN THE red shirt is walking toward the bathroom when she hears a scream. She stops, mere feet from the Indian women she's spent so much of her morning hating, and she looks up the canyon. There's nothing to see but striated stone and the steady glass flumes of the falls. But then she hears another scream, this one issuing from the dark of the canyon like a reckoning, echoing from wall to wall. It's the sharp, jagged sound of life cut down, of death. She trips over herself, falls hard on the wooden bridge. More shouting. Her knee spurts blood. God, she's not ready, she thinks. She's never been ready. She cradles her knee, rocking back and forth on the wood, and feels terror, fresh as the mist, tear through her. Then she sees a woman standing over her. She has a red dot on her forehead and thick white braids of hair. She's kneeling beside her. She's helping her get up and walk to the bench.

"I don't know what's happening," the woman in the red shirt is muttering, "but thank you, thank you!"

Once seated, she grabs the grandmother's arm, squeezing it like a brace.

"God bless ya," she cries. "Here I am making a fool of myself, and you—you rushing to my side like some kind of angel. God bless ya. God bless y'all."

• • •

Randy McFall hears two screams, one after the other, like two shots of a high-caliber pistol separated by time and reflection, by a silent interval that both underscores the reality of the first and leads to the devastation of the second. Then bedlam shouts cluttering the air. Thudding footfalls coming down the mountain.

The ranger races up the stone steps. Adrenaline sears through him like lightning. All the morning's disappointment, the cold faces, the shadowy doubt, is vaporized by the lightning of his movement.

"Up the trail, near that old broke tree!" shouts a ruddy-faced man in a British accent.

"What is it? What happened?"

The ranger's voice is hysterical, almost giddy.

"They jumped off the side," answers a large, sweaty woman who's following the man down. "They fucking jumped! A crazy man and a woman! I think the woman was trying to save him. We have a friend up there who knows 'em. Not really a friend but someone we met this morning."

"Please continue down the trail," the ranger says, whisking his radio from his belt. "Tell anyone you see to head back down, too."

Just as he pushes the transceiver, skipping past the couple, he catches a familiar smell. Body odor. Cheese. The faint and sour tang of alcohol. But no, something else. Deep and pungent and darkly sweet. The smell of sex. He smells sex.

Jesus, he thinks. His finger slips off the radio. He stops mid-trail and watches the rotund couple descend the last few stairs of granite. How? Where? His adrenaline subsides. He feels weak and delirious, like some conspiracy were forming against him, like the screams he heard were precursors to some cruel joke designed to expose him, his loneliness, utterly and forever.

"Dammit," he mumbles.

He sprints up the stairs with fear and anger and hope all mixed up in his stomach.

"Up there, up there," yells a man flying through the stone tunnel like a bat.

Behind the man a blond woman is shuffling two children between the wet and musty walls.

"Wait up, will you?" she shouts at her husband, who's now grabbing the ranger's arm.

"Up there! Where the trail switchbacks! There's a tree!"

The ranger slaps the man's hand.

"Sir, it's a criminal offense to physically accost park personnel."

The man stops stiff as a post, face bewildered beyond any recognizable expression.

"Get going now," the ranger snaps, and he signals for the woman and children to pass. "Now!"

As he exits the tunnel, the ranger's engulfed by yellow, spongy light. The air dense and damp with moisture.

He hurries past a granite wall where purple flowers grow between trail and stone. Then he sees the tree. A broken spire. And a figure standing beside the tree. Filtered sunlight slants across them both. Beyond the edge, in that golden void, billows of mist are coiling like smoke, like spirits, almost invisible if not for the faintest iridescence.

"What happened here?" the ranger asks against the noise of the falls.

Stamer turns to look at him, his face a blank slate.

"I du..." he stammers, "du...don't know."

The ranger approaches the man, registering his identity somewhere in the mess of emotions. He looks over the edge and sees nothing but rock and white water.

"Your friends," he asks, "they jumped?"

Roaring silence. Wet skin. Aching muscles. Objects dumb with gravity.

"Da...Dorle," Stamer manages through tears.

He can't remember the last time he cried.

"Sh...she tried to save him," he says.

He wipes his eyes, realizing in an instant the absurdity of his life. She's gone. Everyone is gone.

"I recognize you," the ranger says. "You're the guy who sat next to me on the bus. Yeah, it's you, isn't it? Well, I told you this place is dangerous. People get hurt all sorts of ways. I told you—"

The ranger feels the flints and sparks of self-assertion die, his judgment whirring in the cold.

"I...I..." now the ranger is stammering.

The sun is breaking through the mist.

"Jesus, I don't know," the ranger gasps. His authority is breaking inside. He can't control it. Something foreign pierces his eyes. He squints as tears fall to the ground. They tinkle in his mind like glass, like pearls pried from the dark, gnarled shell of his pain. Like all the hard, tiny things we carry inside until we can carry them no more.

The ranger can't remember the last time he saw his wife or his children. He wipes his eyes.

"Shit, friend," he says, and this last word rings like light. "Let's get you taken care of, huh?"

He looks over the edge one last time.

"There's nothing for us up here all alone," he says.

Then the ranger takes the stammering man by the arm and leads him down the mountain.

EPILOGUE

I n late summer of 2011, a man drives an old truck, a gray Ford, up Tioga Pass and into the eastern reaches of Yosemite National Park. He stops at Tuolumne Meadows along the river. He parks and gets out of the truck and takes two briefcases from the back. They're jet-black briefcases, the modern hue of business and profit, oddly neat and square against the wild green grasses of the meadow and the loose purple stars of the alpine asters and the grand hunchback shapes of the granite mountains. The tourists in the meadow see a man with a gray beard and watery eyes, wearing a T-shirt, shorts, and sandals. They see a quiet man, someone who's resigned himself to a sense of loss, bar anguish. They think it's strange he carries briefcases, but stranger things have happened in the mountains. Maybe he's a professional photographer. Maybe he's an artist. They watch him for a while as he walks downriver and disappears into a group of pines. They don't see him throw the briefcases into the water. No one notices when he returns less than twenty minutes later with nothing in his hands. He revs the old truck and continues east, climbing toward the Sierra crest and the desert on the other side.

At first, the briefcases float and the cash stays dry. But eventually water finds a way. The cases bob and float downriver as water seeps through their cracks. The cash absorbs a certain amount, but the water keeps coming. Slowly the cases sink to the bottom. The current drags them along until one hits a submerged boulder. The case cracks open and cash whirls out. It's not long until the other case likewise opens, and soon two million dollars are racing down the river. Several of the bills snag on deadfall, flapping against the current. Other bills are sucked into eddies, spinning around as though in a washing machine. All the money will face the river's transformation, one way or another. The water is like a blind institution, exercising its duties with fatal proficiency. Within days, there will be no trace of the cash, its value incorporated back into the natural world. The water will continue downhill and reach the valley checkered with fields. It will reach the edge of the world, where cities bloom in the haze, and men and women try their best to understand the range of light in their lives.

Not far from one of these cities is a small, forgotten town. There's a brick storefront on one of its streets that houses the office of a newspaper. Despite the town's waning population, despite the disappearance of a readership, there is a woman at the newspaper who still writes. She sits at her desk now, mulling over a notebook of inky shorthand, notes she took on a recent trip to the mountains. She's trying to understand something. On her computer screen glows a white blank page, a flashing cursor. She moves to the keyboard and types quickly, stops typing. Two words have broken the blankness: Dorle Wasser. She ponders the name, the face of a woman she knew. And then she writes some more. The words and memories flow like water. She doesn't know which comes first, word or memory, but they flow like water onto her computer screen. They give life to a new story no one has heard before, the story of how an ex-felon, an alcoholic who killed Santa Claus on Christmas Eve, became a hero.

ABOUT THE AUTHOR

Scott Neuffer—author of *Range of Light* and *Scars of the New Order*—is a writer, journalist, poet, and musician who lives in Nevada with his family. His work has appeared in *Nevada Magazine, Foreword Reviews, Underground Voices, Construction Literary Magazine, Shelf Awareness, Entropy Magazine, Wilderness House Literary Review, Gone Lawn*, and elsewhere. He's also the founder and editor of the literary journal *Trampset*. His indie rock music is available on Apple Music and Spotify.

Follow him on Twitter
@scottneuffer @sneuffermusic @trampset

Lightning Source UK Ltd.
Milton Keynes UK
UKHW041206091120
373077UK00016B/1571/J